ALSO BY JEANETTE WINTERSON

THE WORLD
AND OTHER PLACES

THE WORLD
AND OTHER PLACES

Jeanette Winterson

Alfred A. Knopf
New York • Toronto
1999

Copyright © 1998 by Jeanette Winterson
All rights reserved under International and Pan-American
Copyright Conventions. Published in the United States by
Alfred A. Knopf, Inc., New York, and
distributed by Random House, Inc., New York.
Published simultaneously in Canada by Alfred A. Knopf Canada,
a division of Random House of Canada Limited, Toronto, and
distributed by Random House of Canada Limited, Toronto.
www.randomhouse.com

Originally published in Great Britain by Jonathan Cape,
London, in 1998.

Knopf, Borzoi Books, and the colophon are registered
trademarks of Random House, Inc.

Some of the stories in this collection were originally
published as follows: 'The Three Friends' in *Columbia;* 'O'Brien's First
Christmas' in *Elle;* 'Adventure of a Lifetime' in *Esquire;* 'Orion' in
Granta/Home Issue; 'The Poetics of Sex' in *Granta/Best of Young British Writers;*
'Psalms' in *The New Statesman;* and 'The Green Man' and 'Disappearance I'
(originally titled 'Tough Girls Don't Dream') in *The New Yorker.*
'Newton' appeared in the book *The New Gothic,* edited by
Patrick McGrath and Bradford Morrow. 'Atlantic Crossing'
was broadcast on BBC Radio.

Library of Congress Cataloging-in-Publication Data
Winterson, Jeanette.
The world and other places / Jeanette Winterson. — 1st American ed.
p. cm.
ISBN 0-375-40240-3 (alk. paper)
I. Title
PR6073.I558W54 1998
823'.914—dc21   98-28257
CIP

Canadian Cataloguing in Publication Data
Winterson, Jeanette, 1959
The world and other places
ISBN 0-676-97166-0
I. Title
PR6073.I558W67 1998
823'.914   C98-931266-6

Manufactured in the United States of America
First American Edition

To Peggy Reynolds with love

Special thanks to Gary Fisketjon at Knopf
and Suzanne Gluck at ICM

CONTENTS

THE WORLD
AND OTHER PLACES

The 24-Hour Dog

He was soft as rainwater. On that first night I took him across a field mined with pheasants that flew up in our faces when we fused them out. The vertical explosion of a trod pheasant is shock enough when you know it. I knew it and it still skitters me. What could he know at two months old, head like a question mark?

I made him walk on a lead and he jumped for joy, the way creatures do, and children do and adults don't do, and spend their lives wondering where the leap went.

He had the kind of legs that go round in circles. He orbited me. He was a universe of play. Why did I walk so purposefully in a straight line? Where would it take me? He went round and round and we got there all the same.

I had wanted to swim. I had wanted to wash off the hot tyre marks of the day. I wanted to let my body into the obliging water and kick the stars off the surface. I looped my dog-lead through a trough-hoop and undressed. Oh this was fun, a new pair of socks to chew and an old pair of boots to lie on. His questioning head sank to a full stop and he didn't notice me disappear under the water. The night smelled of rosemary and hay.

Oh, this was not fun, his sun drowned and him lost in a dark world without his own name. He started to yap with the wobbly bark he had just discovered and then he discovered he could use his long nose as a Howitzer and fire misery into the fearful place where there had been no fear.

I used my arms as jack levers and raised myself out of the pool. I spoke to him, and he caught the word as deftly as if I had thrown it. This was the edge of time, between chaos and shape. This was the little bit of evolution that endlessly repeats itself in the young and new-born thing. In this moment there are no cars or aeroplanes. The Sistine Chapel is unpainted, no book has been written. There is the moon, the water, the night, one creature's need and another's response. The moment between chaos and shape and I say his name and he hears me.

I had to carry him home, legs folded, nose in my jacket, he was twice as big as a grown cat even now, but small as my arms would allow.

I had collected him that morning from his brothers and sister, his mother, his friends on the farm. He was to be my dog, shot out of a spring litter, a coil of happiness. Bit by bit he would unfold.

He liked my sports car until it moved. Movement to him was four legs or maybe two. He had not yet invented the wheel. He lay behind my neck in stone-age despair, not rigid, but heavy, as his bladder emptied his enterprise, and the blue leather seats were puddled under puppy rain.

We were home in less than five minutes and he staggered from the car as though it were the hold of a slave ship and him left aboard for six months or more. His oversize paws were hesitant on the gravel because he half believed the ground would drive off with him.

I motioned him to the threshold; a little door in a pair of great gates. He looked at me: What should he do? I had to show him that two paws first, two paws after, would jump him across the wooden sill. He fell over but wagged his tail.

I had spent the early morning pretending to be a dog. I had crawled around my kitchen and scullery on all fours at dog height looking for toxic substances (bleach), noxious hazards (boot polish), forbidden delights (rubber boots), death traps (electric wires), swallowables, crunchables, munchables and saw-the-dog-in-half shears and tools.

I had spent the day before putting up new shelving and rearranging the cupboards. A friend from London asked me if I was doing Feng Shui. I had to explain that this was not about energy alignments but somewhere to put the dog biscuits.

I rerouted the washing machine hoses. I had read in my manual that Lurchers like to chew washing machine hoses but only when the machine is on; thus, if they fail to electrocute themselves, they at least succeed in flooding the kitchen.

The week before I had forced my partner to go into Mothercare to purchase a baby gate. The experience nearly killed her. It was not the pastel colours, piped music and cartoon screen, or the assistants, specially graded into mental ages two to four and four to six, or the special offers, one hundred bibs for the price of fifty, it was that she was run down by a fork lift truck moving a consignment of potties.

I fitted the gate. I tried to patch up my relationship. I spent a sleepless night on our new bean bag. I was pretending to be a dog.

The farmer telephoned me the following day.

'Will you come and get him now?'

Now. This now. Not later. Not sooner. Here now. Quick now.

Yes I will come for you. Roll my strength into a ball for you. Throw myself across chance for you. I will be the bridge or the pulley because you are the dream.

He's only a dog. Yes but he will find me out.

Dog and I did the gardening that virgin morning of budding summer. That is, I trimmed the escallonia and he fetched the entire contents of the garage, apart from the car. It began with a pruning gauntlet which he could see I needed. There followed a hanging basket, a Diana Ross cassette, a small fire extinguisher, a handbrush that made him look like Hitler, and one by one a hoarded collection of

Victorian tiles. Being a circular kind of dog he ran in one door to seek the booty and sped out of another to bring it to me. He had not learned the art of braking. When he wanted to stop he just fell over.

I looked at the hoard spread before me. Perhaps this was an exercise in Feng Shui after all. Why did I need a Diana Ross tape? Why was I storing six feet of carpet underlay? I don't have any carpets.

The questions we ask of the universe begin and end with questions like these. He was a cosmic dog.

The light had the quality of water. I was moving through a conscious element. Time is a player. Time is part of today, not simply a measure of its passing.

The dimensionality of time is not usually apparent. I felt it today in the light like water. I knew I was moving through something that had substance. Something serious. Here was the dog, me, the sun, the sky, in a pattern, in a dance, and time was dancing with us, in the motes of light. The day was in the form of us and we were in the form of the day. Time would return it, as memory and as futurity; part of the pattern, the dance that I had refused.

He lay under the table fast asleep while I shelled broad beans. My cats, of which there are four, had taken up sentinel positions on the window ledges. The dog was bottom dog, no doubt, but twice as big as they were. They had not yet understood their psychic advantage. This dog did not know what size he was; he felt tiny to himself. He was still a pocket dog.

I looked at him, trusting, vulnerable, love without caution. He was a new beginning and every new beginning returns the world. In him, the rain forests were pristine and the sea had not been blunted. He was a map of clear outlines and unnamed hope. He was time before or time after. Time now had not spoilt him. In the space between chaos and shape there was another chance.

Night came. We made our journey to the pool. We swam back through the ripples of night. The light wind blew his ears inside out. He whimpered and fell asleep. When I finally staggered him home he was upside down.

I had bought him a bean bag with a purple cover tattooed with bones and chops. Who designs these items and why? What person, living in a town in England, sits down to doodle bones and chops? What kind of a private life does this design suggest? Is it a male or a female?

All these questions had presented themselves but there had been no alternative. A friend had once told me that as soon as she had become a parent, the discriminating good taste of her adult life had been ambushed by a garish crowd of design-bandits. She was finally at the mercy of the retail mob. You want a romper suit? Well, they've all got bunnies on them. You want a doggy bean bag? Well, we cover them in an orgy of chops.

Chops away! Over he went in a somersault of yelping pleasure. Was this really for him? He hurled himself at it and cocked an eye at me from under his paw. Would I shout at him? No! He was a new dog. The world was his bean bag.

I shut the cats in the kitchen with their cat flap. I shut the dog in the scullery with his ball and his bed. I shut myself away in the room that is sleep.

I had read in my manual that a dog must be dominated. He must not sleep upstairs. He must sleep alone.

An hour later I woke up. I understood that my dog had not read the manual. He told this to the night in long wails. I did not know what I should do and so I did nothing. He had been used to sleeping in a heap with his brothers and sister. Now he was alone. He called and kept calling and this time I did not answer. Chaos was complete.

About nine o'clock I went downstairs into the kitchen. The cats were on their perches, glaring at me with bags under their eyes like a set of Louis Vuitton luggage.

'We're leaving home,' they said. 'Just give us our breakfast and we're off.'

I fed them and they queued up at the cat flap like a column of ants.

I glanced in the mirror. The bags under my eyes needed a porter's trolley.

Next question. The dog?

I opened the door into the scullery. The dog was lying on his bean bag, nose in his paws, a sight of infinite dejection. I stood for a moment, then he unsteadily got up and crawled across the floor to me on his belly. As anticipated by the manual, I had become the master.

I let him out into the sunlight. I gave him his gigantic bowl of cereal and milk. I have always loved the way dogs eat their food; the splashy, noisy, hog pleasure of head in trough. I am a great supporter of table manners but it is worthwhile to be reminded of what we are.

And that was the problem; the dog would pour through me and every pin hole would be exposed. I know I am a leaky vessel but do I want to know it every day?

He's only a dog. Yes but he has found me out.

. . .

I clipped on his lead and walked him round the fields in my dressing gown and boots. If this seems eccentric, remember that my soul had been exposed and whatever I wore was of no use to cover it. Why dress when I could not be clothed?

He circled along in his warm skin, happy again because he was free and because he belonged. All of one's life is a struggle towards that; the narrow path between freedom and belonging. I have sometimes sacrificed freedom in order to belong, but more often I have given up all hope of belonging.

It is no use trying to assume again the state of innocence and acceptance of the animal or the child. This time it has to be conscious. To circle about in such gladness as his, is the effort of a whole lifetime.

The day was misty and settled on his coat like a warning. I was looking into the future, thinking about what I would have to be to the dog in return for what he would be to me. It would have been much easier if he had been an easier dog. I mean, less intelligent, less sensitive, less brimful of that *jouissance* which should not be harmed.

It would have been much easier if I had been an easier person. We were so many edges, dog and me, and of the same recklessness. And of the same love. I have learned what love costs. I never count it but I know what it costs.

.   .   .

I telephoned the farmer. 'You will have to take him back,' I said. 'I can't do this.'

It had been the arrangement between us from the start; when there were six puppies in a squealing heap and one by one sensible country people had come to claim them. There is no reason why I should not keep a dog. I have enough land, enough house, enough time, and patience with whatever needs to grow.

I had thought about everything carefully before I had agreed to him. I had made every preparation, every calculation, except for those two essentials that could not be calculated; his heart and mine.

My girlfriend carried the bean bag. I walked the dog, gaiety in the bounce of him, his body spinning as the planet spins, this little round of life.

We were escorted off the premises by my venerable cat, an ancient, one-eyed bugger of a beast, of whom the dog was afraid. At the boundary of our field, the cat sat, as he always does, waiting for us to come back, this time by ourselves.

As we reached the farm, the dog hesitated and hung his head. I spoke to him softly. I tried to explain. I don't know what he understood but I knew he understood that he would not be my dog anymore. We were crossing an invisible line high as a fence.

For the last time I picked him up and carried him.

Then of course there was his mother and his brothers and sister and I gave them biscuits and bones and the bean bag was a badge of pride for him. Look what he had been and got.

We put him in the run and he began to play again, over and tumble in a simple doggy way, and already the night, the pool, the wind, his sleeping body, the misty morning that had lain on us both, were beginning to fade.

I don't know what the farmer thought. I mumbled the suitable excuses, and it was true that my partner had just heard she would be working away for some weeks, and that it is tough to manage one's own work, the land, the house, the animals, even without a brand-new dog.

What I couldn't say was that the real reason was so much deeper and harder and that we spend our lives deceiving ourselves of those real reasons, perhaps because when they are clear they are too painful.

I used to hear him barking in the weeks that followed. His bark aimed at my heart. Then another person claimed him and called him Harry, and took him to live on a farm where there were children and ducks and company and things to do and the kind of doggy life he never would have had with me. What would I have done? Taught him to read?

I know he won't be the dog he could have been if I had met him edge to edge, his intensity and mine. Maybe it's better that way. Maybe it's better for me. I live in the space between chaos and shape. I walk the line that continually threatens to lose its tautness under me, dropping me into the dark pit where there is no meaning. At other times the line is so wired that it lights up the soles of my feet, gradually my whole body, until I am my own beacon, and I see then the beauty of newly created worlds, a form that is not random. A new beginning.

I saw all this in him and it frightened me.

I gave him a name. It was Nimrod, the mighty hunter of Genesis, who sought out his quarry and brought it home. He found me out. I knew he would. The strange thing is that although I have given him away, I can't lose him, and he can't die. There he is, forever, part of the pattern, the dance, and running beside me, joyful.

Atlantic Crossing

I met Gabriel Angel in 1956. The year Arthur Miller married Marilyn Monroe. I was going home. Gabriel Angel was leaving home. We were both going to the same place. We were going to London. The Millers were there too at the time.

The *Cowdenbeath* was a pre-war liner with a mahogany lining. She looked like a bath-time boat with two fat black funnels and a comfortable way of sitting in the water. She had been money and ease, the Nancy Astor generation, not the frugal fifties.

She had been requisitioned as a troop ship during the war, and now her cruising days were over, she was faded, just a ferry, when I got to her. Once a month she sailed from Southampton to St Lucia and once a month she sailed back again. One end of the bath to the other in eight days. She didn't have glamour but she had plenty of stories to tell and I've always liked that in a woman. It is what I liked about Gabriel Angel.

Journeys make me nervous, so I was up too early on the morning of my leaving, opening and shutting my trunk and bothering the porters about safe storage. The gangway up to the *Cowdenbeath* was busy with bodies run random like ants before ants. There was freight to be loaded, food to get on board, everything to be cleared before eleven o'clock embarkation.

Invisible worlds, or worlds that are supposed to be invisible interest me. I like to see the effort it takes for some people to make things go smoothly for other people. Don't misunderstand me; mostly I'm part of the invisible world myself.

A couple of hours after I had permanently creased my permanent press suit by sitting hunched up in a roll of rope, I saw a good-looking black woman, maybe twenty, maybe twenty-five, standing with her feet together, a little brown suitcase in her hand. She was staring at the boat as if she intended to buy it. If the sea hadn't been on one side, she would have walked right round, her head cocked like a spaniel, her eyes eager and thoughtful.

After a few moments she was joined by a much older woman with a particular dignity. The younger one said something to her, then spread out her arm towards the ship. Whatever it was, they both laughed, which did nothing for my nerves. I wanted to be reassured by the imposing vessel before me, not have it picked at like a cotton bale.

I climbed out of my rope hole, grabbed my hat, and sauntered towards them. They didn't give me a glance, but I heard the older one asking to be sent a tin of biscuits with a picture of the Queen on the lid. It is the same all over the Commonwealth; they all love the latest Queen. She's too young for me.

. . .

The steward showed me to my cabin. Mr Duncan Stewart D22. I opened my hand luggage, spread a few things on the lower bunk, and went back up on deck to watch the spectacle. I like to see the people arriving. I like to imagine their lives. It keeps me from thinking too much about my own. A man shouldn't be too introspective. It weakens him. That is the difference between Tennessee Williams and Ernest Hemingway. I'm a Hemingway man myself although I don't believe it is right to hunt lions.

Look at these two coming on deck right now; lesbians I'll bet. Both about sixty-five, shrunk into their cotton suits and wearing ancient Panamas. The stout one has a face the colour and texture of a cricket ball and the thin one looks as if she's been folded once too often.

What brogues the stout one is wearing; polished like conkers and laced too tight. Shoe lacing is a revealing and personal matter. There are criss-cross lacers; the neat brisk people who like a pattern under the surface. There are straight-lacers; who pretend to be tougher than they are but when they come undone, boy, are they undone. There are the tie-tights; the ones who need to feel secure, and there are the slack-jacks, who like to leave themselves a little loose, the ones who would rather not wear shoes at all. I've met people who always use a double knot. They are liars. I'm telling you because I know.

. . .

Once the lesbians had gone by, trailing their old woman smell of heavy scent and face powder, I went back downstairs, intending to nap for an hour. I was suddenly very tired. I wanted to get my jacket off, let my feet smell, and wake up an hour later to a Scotch and Soda. In my mind I was through the sleep and tasting the drink.

I opened the door to my cabin. There was the young woman I had noticed earlier on the dock. She turned at the noise of the door and looked surprised.

'Can I help you?' she said.

'There must be some mistake,' I said, 'this is my cabin.' She frowned and picked up a cabin list from the top of her little suitcase. Her voice lilted.

'D22. G Angel and D Stewart.'

'That's right. I am Duncan Stewart.'

'And I am Gabriel Angel.'

'You should be a man.'

She looked confused and examined herself in the mirror. I tried to pursue this obvious line. Obvious to me.

'Gabriel is a man's name.'

'Gabriel is an angel's name,' she said.

'Angels are men. Look at Raphael and Michael.'

'Look at Gabriel.'

I did look at her. No wings but great legs. Still, I was tired and did not want to argue theology with a young woman I had never met. I thought about the bunk and the Scotch and started feeling sorry for myself. I decided to go and tackle the Purser.

'You stay here until I get back,' I commanded, 'I'll straighten it out.'

I didn't straighten it out. The ship was crammed to the lifeboats. The Purser, like me, like any normal person guided by Bible basics, had assumed Gabriel was a man's name. That's why we had been yoked together. Second Class ticket holders can't be choosy. I had to explain all this to her but she didn't flinch. Either she was as innocent as she looked or she was an old hand. Some of these girls have been milking men since breast-swell. I didn't want any trouble.

'Top or bottom?' I asked, getting ready to move my stuff.

'Top,' she said. 'I like heights.'

She climbed up and lay down and I eased myself below, keeping my shoes on, in case my feet smelled. I was disappointed. I had expected to share but I had hoped for some tough guy who wanted late night Scotch and a pack of cards. When you dig under the surface, past the necessities, men and women don't mix.

Her head came dipping over the side of the bunk.

'Are you asleep?'

'Yes.'

'So am I.'

There was a pause, then she asked me what I did for a living.

'I'm a business man. I do business.'

She was looking at me upside down, like a big brown bat. She was making me feel sea-sick.

'What about you?' I said, not caring.

'I'm an aviator.'

Eight days at sea. One day longer than God needed to invent the whole world, including its holiday pattern. Two days longer than he took to make her Grandmother Eve and my Grandfather Adam. This time I am not falling for the apple.

We sat up on deck today, Gabriel Angel and myself. She told me she was born in 1937, the day that Amelia Earhart had become the first woman to complete the Atlantic crossing, solo flight. Her granddaddy, as she calls him, told her it was an omen, and that's why they called her Gabriel, 'bringer of Good News,' a bright flying thing.

Her granddaddy taught her to fly in the mail planes he ran between the islands. He told her she had to be smarter than life, find a way of beating gravity, and to believe in herself as angels do, their bodies bright as dragonflies, great gold wings cut across the sun.

I'm not against anyone fastening their life to an event of some significance and that way making themselves significant. God knows, we need what footholds we can find on the glass mountain of our existence. Trouble is, you climb and climb, and around middle age, you discover you have spent all the time in the same spot. You thought you were going to be somebody until you slip down into the nobody that you are. I'm telling you because I know.

She said, 'I am poor but even the poorest inherit something, their daddy's eyes, their mother's courage. I inherited the dreams.'

I leaned back. I could see in her a piece of the bright hope I once had in myself and it made me sour and angry. It made me feel sorry for her too. I wanted to take both her hands in mine, look her in the eye, and let her see that the world isn't interested in a little black girl's dreams.

She said, 'Mr Stewart, have you ever been in love?' She was leaning over the side, watching the ocean. I watched the curve of her spine, the slender tracings of her hips beneath her dress. I wanted to touch her. I don't know why. She's too young for me.

Before I could answer, although I don't know how I would have answered, she started talking about a man with stars in his hair and arms stretched out like wings to hold her.

I moved away as soon as I could.

.   .   .

What is there to say about love? You could sweep up all the words and stack them in the gutter and love wouldn't be any different, wouldn't feel any different, the hurt in the heart, the headachy desire that hardly submits to language. What we can't tame we talk about. I'm talking a lot about Gabriel Angel.

If I were able to speak the truth, I'd say I had a fiancée before the War, and we're going back to 1938 now. She had a thick plait of hair that ran all the way down her back. She could wrap her hair around her as though it were a snake. I was no snake charmer.

She was a farmer's daughter, had a heart like a tractor to pull any man out of himself. Her hair was red the way the sun is red first thing in the morning. She had a look about her that took everything seriously, even the wood pile. There were plenty of men who would have traded their bodies for a split log, just to be under her hands for five minutes. I know I would. We didn't touch much. She didn't seem to want it. When we said goodnight at the bottom of her lane she let me run my index finger from her temple to her throat. Such soft hair she had on her face, invisible, but not to my hand.

If I were young again, I would have bounced up to Gabriel Angel on the dock and asked her to come with me on the later sailing. That would have been the Italian line, the real cruise ship. SS *Garibaldi* softly rocking the Mediterranean. Forget the direct Atlantic crossing, carrying workers and immigrants to a cold place they've never seen. I could have held her hand through Martinique, Las Palmas, Tenerife. I could have put my arm around her waist through the straits of Gibraltar. At Barcelona I would have bought her gem Madonnas and seed pearls. Then we would have continued by sea to Genoa and met the boat-train for England. That railway, through Italy, Switzerland and France, was laid in the 1850s and was one of the first to be constructed. I'm told that Robert Browning, poet, and Mrs Elizabeth Barrett Browning, also poet, travelled along its length. I would have enjoyed that connection. I should like to run away with Gabriel Angel.

As it is, we're on this ferry boat to Southampton, the short direct brutal route, and Gabriel Angel has never been in my arms.

It turns out that the two lesbians are missionaries. Miss Bead, the one with a face like a love-note somebody crushed in his fist, tells me they have been in Trinidad for thirty years. Miss Quim, the cricket ball, has taught three generations of hockey teams. They are on their way home to buy a farmhouse together in Wales and get a dog called Rover. I realise they are happy.

I am not sleeping well. Below my cabin is dormitory accommodation, the cheapest way to travel. That's all right, what's wrong is the Barbados Banjo Band, twenty-five of them, on their way to the dancehalls of England. It isn't easy to sleep well piled on top of fifty feet, five hundred fingers and toes and forty-six eyes. Above me are the maddening curves of Gabriel Angel.

In the ship's lounge, proudly displayed, is a large map of the Atlantic, threaded through with the red line of our route. Every day one of the stewards moves a gay green flag further along the red line, so that we can see where we are. Today we have reached the middle; the point of no return. Today the future is nearer than the past.

I don't have anyone to go to in England. No one will be waiting for me at Southampton or Victoria. I have a two-bedroomed terraced house in London. I have had it let for the past twelve years and I'll have to live in a boarding house until it becomes vacant again next month. I won't recognise anything familiar. I had the agents furnish it cheaply for me.

Later, my cargo will arrive and I'll start selling Caribbean crafts and trinkets and I suppose I'll go on doing that until something better comes along or until I die. Looking at my future is like looking at a rainy day through a dirty window.

'You must be excited, Mr Stewart.'

'What about, Miss Angel?'

She has been reading my copy of *Wuthering Heights* by

Emily Brontë: and now she wishes she could live in Yorkshire. I must be careful not to lend her *Rob Roy*.

Is compassion possible between a man and a woman? When I say (as I have not said), 'I want to take care of you,' do I mean 'I want you to take care of me'?

I am materially comfortable. I can provide. I could protect. I have a lot to offer a young woman in a strange place without friends or money.

'Will you marry me, Miss Angel?'

It is early in the morning, not yet six o'clock. I have dressed carefully. My tie is even and my shoes are well polished and double knotted. Anyone can look at me now. Up on deck the sea chops at the boat, the waves are like grey icing, forked over. The wind is whipping my coat sleeves and making my eyes water.

Today we will dock at Southampton and I will catch the train to Victoria station and shake hands with my fellow travellers and we will wish each other well and forget each other at once. I think I'll spend tonight in a good hotel.

Last night I could not sleep, so I climbed the bunk ladder and stared at Gabriel Angel, lying peacefully under the dim yellow safety lamp. Why doesn't she want me?

The sun is rising now, but it is 93,000,000 miles away

and I can't get warm. Soon Gabriel Angel will come on deck in her short sleeved blouse and carrying a pair of borrowed binoculars. She won't be cold. She has the sun inside her.

I wish the wind would drop. A man looks silly with tears in his eyes.

The Poetics of Sex

Why Do You Sleep with Girls?

My lover Picasso is going through her Blue Period. In the past her periods have always been red. Radish red, bull red, red like rose hips bursting seed. Lava red when she was called Pompeii and in her Destructive Period. The stench of her, the brack of her, the rolling splitting cunt of her. Squat like a Sumo, ham thighs, loins of pork, beefy upper cuts and breasts of lamb. I can steal her heart like a bird's egg.

  She rushes for me bull-subtle, butching at the gate as if she's come to stud. She bellows at the window, bloods the pavement with desire. She says, 'You don't need to be Rapunzel to let down your hair.' I know the game. I know enough to flick my hind-quarters and skip away. I'm not a flirt. She can smell the dirt on me and that makes her swell. That's what makes my lithe lover bulrush-thin fat me. How she fats me. She plumps me, pats me, squeezes and feeds me. Feeds me up with lust till I'm as fat as she is. We're fat for each other we sapling girls. We neat clean branching girls get thick with sex. You are wide enough for my hips like roses, I will cover you with my petals, cover you with the scent of me. Cover girl wide for the weight of my cargo. My bull-lover makes a matador out of me. She circles me and in her rough-made ring I am complete. I like the dressing up, the little jackets, the silk tights, I like her shiny hide, the deep tanned leather of her. It is she who gives me the power of the sword. I used it once but when I cut at her it was my close fit flesh that frilled into a hem of blood. She lay beside me slender as a horn. Her little jacket and silk tights impeccable. I sweated muck and couldn't speak in my broken ring. We are quick change artists we girls.

Which One of You Is the Man?

Picasso's veins are Kingfisher blue and Kingfisher shy. The first time I slept with her I couldn't see through the marble columns of her legs or beyond the opaque density of each arm. A sculptor by trade, Picasso is her own model.

The blue that runs through her is sanguine. One stroke of the knife and she changes colour. Every month and she changes colour. Deep pools of blue silk drop from her. I know her by the lakes she leaves on the way to the bedroom. Her braces cascade over the stair-rail, she wears earrings of lapis lazuli which I have caught cup-handed, chasing her *deshabillée*.

When she sheds she sheds it all. Her skin comes away with her clothes. On those days I have been able to see the blood-depot of her heart. On those days it was possible to record the patience of her digestive juices and the relentlessness of her lungs. Her breath is blue in the cold air. She breathes into the blue winter like a Madonna of the Frost. I think it right to kneel and the view is good.

She does perform miracles but they are of the physical kind and ordered by her Rule of Thumb to the lower regions. She goes among the poor with every kind of salve unmindful of reward. She dresses in blue she tells me so that they will know she is a saint and it is saintly to taste the waters of so many untried wells.

I have been jealous of course. I have punished her good deeds with some alms-giving of my own. It's not the answer, I can't catch her by copying her, I can't draw her with a borrowed stencil. She is all the things a lover should be and quite a few a lover should not. Pin her down? She's not a butterfly. I'm not a wrestler. She's not a target. I'm not a gun. Tell you what she is? She's not Lot no. 27 and I'm not one to brag.

We were by the sea yesterday and the sea was heavy with salt so that our hair was braided with it. There was salt on our hands and in our wounds where we'd been fighting. 'Don't hurt me,' I said and I unbuttoned my shirt so that she could look at my breasts if she wanted to. 'I'm no saint,' she said and that was true, true too that our feet are the same size. The rocks were reptile blue and the sky that balanced on the top of the cliffs was sheer blue. Picasso made me put on her jersey and drink dark tea from a fifties flask.

'It's winter,' she said. 'Let's go.'

We did go, leaving the summer behind, leaving a trail of footprints two by two in identical four. I don't know that anyone behind could have told you which was which and if they had there would have been no trace by morning.

What Do Lesbians Do in Bed?

Under cover of the sheets the tabloid world of lust and vice is useful only in so much as Picasso can wipe her brushes on it. Beneath the sheets we practise Montparnasse, that is Picasso offers to paint me but we have sex instead.

We met at Art School on a shiny corridor. She came towards me so swiftly that the linoleum dissolved under her feet. I thought, 'A woman who can do that to an oil cloth can certainly do something for me.' I made the first move. I took her by her pony tail the way a hero grabs a runaway horse. She was taken aback. When she turned round I kissed her ruby mouth and took a sample of her sea blue eyes. She was salty, well preserved, well made and curved like a wave. I thought, 'This is the place to go surfing.'

We went back to her studio, where naturally enough, there was a small easel and a big bed. 'My work comes first,' she said. 'Would you mind?' and not waiting for an answer she mixed an ochre wash before taking me like a dog my breasts hanging over the pillow.

Not so fast Picasso, I too can rumple you like a farm hand, roll you like good tobacco leaf against my thighs. I can take that arrogant throat and cut it with desire. I can make you dumb with longing, tease you like a doxy on a date.

Slowly now Picasso, where the falling light hits the floor. Lie with me in the bruised light that leaves dark patches on your chest. You look tubercular, so thin and mottled, quiescent now. I picked you up and carried you to the bed dusty with ill-use. I found a newspaper under the sheets advertising rationing.

The girl on the canvas was sulky. She hadn't come to be painted. I'd heard all about you my tear-away tiger, so fierce, so unruly. But the truth is other as truth always is. What holds the small space between my legs is not your artistic tongue nor any of the other parts you play at will but the universe beneath the sheets that we make together.

We are in our igloo and it couldn't be snugger. White on white on white on white. Sheet Picasso me sheet. Who's on top depends on where you're standing but as we're lying down it doesn't matter. What an Eskimo I am, breaking her seductive ice and putting in my hand for fish. How she wriggles, slithers, twists to resist me but I can bait her and I do. A fine catch, one in each hand and one in my mouth. Impressive for a winter afternoon and the stove gone out and the rent to pay. We are warm and rich and white. I have so much enjoyed my visit.

'Come again?' she asked. Yes tomorrow, under the sodium street lights, under the tick of the clock. Under my obligations, my history, my fears, this now. This fizzy, giddy all consuming now. I will not let time lie to me. I will not listen to dead voices or unborn pain. 'What if?' has no power

against 'What if not?' The not of you is unbearable. I must
have you. Let them prate, those scorn-eyed anti-romantics.
Love is not the oil and I am not the machine. Love is you
and here I am. Now.

Were You Born a Lesbian?

Picasso is an unlikely mother but I owe myself to her. We
are honour-bound, love-bound, bound by cords too robust
for those healthy hospital scissors. She baptised me from
her own font and said, 'I name thee Sappho.' People often
ask if we are mother and child.

I could say yes, I could say no, both statements would be
true, the way that lesbians are true, at least to one another if
not to the world. I am no stranger to the truth but very
uncomfortable about the lies that have dogged me since my
birth. It is no surprise that we do not always remember our
name.

I am proud to be Picasso's lover in spite of the queer
looks we get when holding hands on busy streets. 'Mummy,
why is that man staring at us?' I said when only one month
old. 'Don't worry dear, he can't help it, he's got something
wrong with his eyes.'

We need more Labradors. The world is full of blind people. They don't see Picasso and me dignified in our love.
They see perverts, inverts, tribades, homosexuals. They see
circus freaks and Satan worshippers, girl-catchers and

porno turn-ons. Picasso says they don't know how to look at pictures either.

Were You Born a Lesbian?

A fairy in a pink tutu came to Picasso and said, 'I bring you tidings of great joy. All by yourself with no one to help you you will give birth to a sex toy who has a way with words. You will call her Sappho and she will be a pain in the ass to all men.'

'Can't you see I've got a picture to finish?' said Picasso.

'Take a break,' said the fairy. 'There's more to life than Art.'

'Where?' said Picasso, whose first name wasn't Mary.

'Between your legs,' said Gabriel.

'Forget it. Don't you know I paint with my clit?'

'Here, try a brush,' said the fairy offering her a fat one.

'I've had all the brushes I need,' said Picasso.

'Too Late,' said the fairy. 'Here she comes.'

Picasso slammed the door on her studio and ran across to the Art College where she had to give a class. She was angry so that her breath burnt the air. She was angry so that her feet dissolved the thin lino tiles already scuffed to ruin by generations of brogues. There was no one in the corridor or if there was she was no one. Picasso didn't recognise her, she had her eyes on the door and the door looked away. Picasso, running down the clean corridor, was suddenly trip-wired, badly thrown, her hair came away from her glorious head. She was being scalped. She was being mugged. She was detonated on a long fuse of sex. Her body was half way out of the third floor window and there was a demon against her mouth. A poker-red pushing babe crying, 'Feed me, Feed me now.'

Picasso took her home, what else could she do? She took her home to straighten her out and had her kinky side up. She mated with this creature she had borne and began to feel that maybe the Greek gods knew a thing or two. Flesh of her flesh she fucked her.

They were quiet then because Sappho hadn't learned a language. She was still two greedy hands and an open mouth. She throbbed like an outboard motor, she was as sophisticated as a ham sandwich. She had nothing to offer but herself, and Picasso, who thought she had seen it all before, smiled like a child and fell in love.

Why Do You Hate Men?

Here comes Sappho, scorching the history books with tongues of flame. Never mind the poetry feel the erection. Oh yes, women get erect, today my body is stiff with sex. When I see a word held hostage to manhood I have to rescue it. Sweet trembling word, locked in a tower, tired of your Prince coming and coming. I will scale you and discover that size is no object especially when we're talking inches.

I like to be a hero, like to come back to my island full of girls carrying a net of words forbidden them. Poor girls, they are locked outside their words just as the words are locked into meaning. Such a lot of locking up goes on on the Mainland but here the doors are always open.

Stay inside, don't walk the streets, bar the windows, keep your mouth shut, keep your legs together, strap your purse around your neck, don't wear valuables, don't look up, don't talk to strangers, don't risk it, don't try it. He means she except when it means Men. This is a Private Club.

That's all right boys, so is this. This delicious unacknowledged island where we are naked with each other. The boat that brings us here will crack beneath your weight. This is territory you cannot invade. We lay on the bed, Picasso and I, listening to the terrible bawling of Salami. Salami is a male artist who wants to be a Lesbian.

'I'll pay you twice the rent,' he cries, fingering his greasy wallet.

'I'll paint you for posterity. I love women, don't you know? Oh God I wish I was a woman, wafer-thin like you, I could circle you with one hand.' He belches.

Picasso is unimpressed. She says, 'The world is full of heterosexuals, go and find one, half a dozen, swallow them like oysters, but get out.'

'Oh whip me,' says Salami getting moist.

We know the pattern. In half an hour he'll be violent and when he's threatened us enough, he'll go to the sleaze pit and watch two girls for the price of a steak.

As soon as he left we forgot about him. Making love we made a dictionary of forbidden words. We are words, sentences, stories, books. You are my New Testament. We are a gospel to each other, I am your annunciation, revelation. You are my St Mark, winged lion at your feet. I'll have you, and the lion too, buck under you till you learn how to saddle me. Don't dig those spurs too deep. It's not so simple this lexographic love. When you have sunk me to the pit I'll mine you in return and we shall be husbands to each other as well as wives.

I'll tell you something Salami, a woman can get hard and keep it there all night and when she's not required to stand she knows how to roll. She can do it any way up and her lover always comes. There are no frigid lesbians, think of that.

On this island where we live, keeping what we do not tell, we have found the infinite variety of Woman. On the Mainland, Woman is largely extinct in all but a couple of obvious forms. She is still cultivated as a cash crop but is nowhere to be found growing wild.

Salami hates to hear us fuck. He bangs on the wall like a zealot at an orgy. 'Go home,' we say, but he doesn't. He'd rather lie against the skirting board complaining that we stop him painting. The real trouble is that we have rescued a word not allowed to our kind.

He hears it pounding through the wall day and night. He smells it on our clothes and sees it smeared on our faces. We are happy Picasso and I. Happy.

Don't You Find There's Something Missing?

I thought I had lost Picasso. I thought the bright form that shapes my days had left me. I was loose at the edges, liquid with uncertainty. The taut lines of love slackened. I felt myself unravelling backwards, away from her. Would the thinning thread snap?

For seven years she and I had been in love. Love between lovers, love between mother and child. Love between man and wife. Love between friends. I had been all of those things to her and she had been all of those things to me. What we were we were in equal parts, and twin souls to one another. We like to play roles but we know who we are. You are beauty to me Picasso. Not only sensuous beauty that pleases the eye but artistic beauty that challenges it. Sometimes you are ugly in your beauty, magnificently ugly and you frighten me for all the right reasons.

I did not tell you this yesterday or the day before. Habit had silenced me the way habit does. So used to a thing no need to speak it, so well known the action no need to describe it. But I know that speech is freedom which is not the same as freedom of speech. I have no right to say what I please when I please but I have the gift of words with which to bless you. Bless you Picasso. Bless you for your straight body like a spire. You are the landmark that leads me through the streets of the everyday. You take me past the little houses towards the church where we worship. I do worship you because you are worthy of praise. Bless you Picasso for your able hands that carry the paint to the unbirthed canvas. Your fingers were red when you fucked me and my body striped with joy. I miss the weals of our passion just as I miss the daily tenderness of choosing you. Choosing you above all others, my pearl of great price.

My feelings for you are biblical; that is they are intense, reckless, arrogant, risky and unconcerned with the way of the world. I flaunt my bleeding wounds, madden with my certainty. The Kingdom of Heaven is within you Picasso. Bless you.

There is something missing and that is you. Your clothes were gone yesterday, your easel was packed flat and silent against the wall. When I got up and left our unmade bed there was the smell of coffee in the house but not the smell of you. I looked in the mirror and I knew who was to blame. Why take the perfect thing and smash it? Some goods are smashed that cannot be replaced.

It has been difficult this last year. Love is difficult. Love gets harder which is not the same as to say that it gets harder to love. You are not hard to love. You are hard to love well. Your standards are high, you won't settle for the quick way out which is why you made for the door. If I am honest I will admit that I have always wanted to avoid love. Yes give me romance, give me sex, give me fights, give me all the parts of love but not the simple single word which is so complex and demands the best of me this hour this minute this forever.

Picasso won't paint the same picture twice. She says develop or die. She won't let yesterday's love suffice for today. She makes it new, she remixes her colours and stretches her canvas until it sighs. My mother was glad when she heard we'd split up. She said, 'Now you can come back to the Mainland. I'll send Phaeon to pick you up.' Phaeon runs a little business called LESBIAN TOURS. He drives his motor-boat round and round the island, just outside the one mile exclusion zone. He points out famous lesbians to sight-seers who always say, 'But she's so attractive!' or 'She's so ugly!'

'Yeah,' says Phaeon, 'and you know what? They're all in love with me.' One sight-seer shakes his head like a collecting box for a good cause. 'Can't you just ask one of 'em?' he says. 'I can ask them anything,' says Phaeon who never waits to hear the answer.

Why Do You Sleep with Girls?

Picasso has loved me for fifty years and she loves me still. We got through the charcoal tunnel where the sun stopped rising. We no longer dress in grey.

On that day I told you about I took my coat and followed her footprints across the ice. As she walked the world froze up behind her. There was nothing for me to return to, if I failed, I failed alone. Despair made it too dark to see, I had to travel by radar, tracking her warmth in front of me. It's fashionable now to say that any mistake is made by both of you. That's not always true. One person can easily kill another.

Hang on me my darling like rubies round my neck. Slip onto my finger like a ring. Give me your rose for my button-hole. Let me leaf through you before I read you out loud.

Picasso warms my freezing heart on the furnace of her belly. Her belly is stoked to blazing with love of me. I have learned to feed her every day, to feed her full of fuel that I gladly find. I have unlocked the storehouses of love. On the Mainland they teach you to save for a rainy day. The truth is that love needs no saving. It is fresh or not at all. We are fresh and plentiful. She is my harvest and I am hers. She seeds me and reaps me, we fall into one another's laps. Her seas are thick with fish for my rod. I have rodded her through and through.

She is painting today. The room is orange with effort. She is painting today and I have written this.

The Three Friends

Once upon a time there were two friends who found a third. Liking no one better in the whole world, they vowed to live in one palace, sail in one ship, and fight one fight with equal arms.

After three months they decided to go on a quest.

'What shall we seek?' they asked each other.

The first said, 'Gold.'

The second said, 'Wives.'

The third said, 'That which cannot be found.'

They all agreed that this last was best and so they set off in fine array.

After a while they came to a house that celebrated ceilings and denied floors. As they marched through the front door they were only just in time to save themselves from dropping into a deep pit. While they clung in terror to the wainscotting, they looked up and saw chandeliers, bright as swords, that hung and glittered and lit the huge room where the guests came to and fro. The room was arranged for dinner, tables and chairs suspended from great chains. An armoury of knives and forks laid out in case the eaters knocked one into the abyss.

There was a trumpet sound and the guests began to enter the room through a trap door in the ceiling. Some were suspended on wires, others walked across ropes slender as youth. In this way they were all able to join their place setting. When all were assembled, the trumpet blew again, and the head of the table looked down and said to the three friends, 'What is it you seek?'

'That which cannot be found.'

'It is not here,' she answered, 'but take some gold,' and each of the diners threw down a solid gold plate, rather in the manner that the Doge of Venice used to throw his dinnerware into the canal to show how much he despised worldly things.

Our three friends did not despise worldly things, and caught as many of the plates as they could. Loaded down with treasure they continued on their way, though more slowly than before.

Eventually they came to Turkey, and to the harem of Mustapha the Blessed CIXX. Blessed he was, so piled with ladies, that only his index finger could be seen. Crooking it he bade the friends come forward, and asked in a muffled voice, 'What is it you seek?'

'That which cannot be found.'

'It is not here,' he said in a ghostly smother, 'but take some wives.'

The friends were delighted, but observing the fate of Mustapha, they did not take too many. Each took six and made them carry the gold plate.

Helter skelter down the years the friends continued their journey, crossing continents of history and geography, gathering by chance the sum of the world, so that nothing was missing that could be had.

At last they came to a tower in the middle of the sea. A man with the face of centuries and the voice of the wind opened a narrow window and called,

'What is it you seek?'

'That which cannot be found . . . found . . . found' and the wind twisted their voices into the air.

'It has found you,' said the man.

They heard a noise behind them like a scythe cutting the water and when they looked they saw a ship thin as a blade gaining towards them. The figure rowed it standing up, with one oar that was not an oar. They saw the curve of the metal flashing, first this side and then that. They saw the rower throw back his hood. They saw him beckon to them and the world tilted. The sea poured away.

Who are they with fish and starfish in their hair?

Orion

Here are the coordinates: Five hours, thirty minutes right ascension (the coordinate on the celestial sphere analogous to longitude on earth) and zero declination (at the celestial equator). Any astronomer can tell where you are.

It's different, isn't it, from head back in the garden on a frosty night, sensing other worlds through a pair of binoculars? I like those nights; kitchen light out, wearing Wellingtons with shiny silver insoles. On the wrapper there is a picture of an astronaut showing off his shiny silver suit. A short trip to the moon has brought some comfort back to earth. We can wear what Neil Armstrong wore and never feel the cold. This must be good news for star-gazers whose feet are firmly on the ground. We have moved with the times. And so will Orion.

Every 200,000 years or so, the individual stars within each constellation shift position. That is, they are shifting all the time, but more subtly than any tracker dog of ours can follow. One day, if the earth has not voluntarily opted out of the solar system we will wake up to a new heaven whose dome will again confound us. It will still be home but not a place to take for granted. I wouldn't be able to tell you the story of Orion and say, 'Look, there he is, and there's his dog Sirius whose loyalty has left him bright.'

The dot-to-dot log book of who we were is not a fixed text.

For Orion, who was the result of three of the gods in a good mood pissing on an ox-hide, the only tense he recognised was the future continuous. He was a mighty hunter. His arrow was always in flight, his prey, endlessly just ahead of him. The carcasses he left behind became part of his past faster than they could decay. When he went to Crete he did no sunbathing. He rid the island of all its wild beasts. He could really swing a cudgel.

Stories abound: Orion was so tall he could walk along the sea bed without wetting his hair. So strong he could part a mountain. He wasn't the kind of man who settles down. And then he met Artemis, who wasn't the kind of woman who settles down either. They were both hunters and both gods. Their meeting is recorded in the heavens, but you can't see it every night, only on certain nights of the year. The rest of the time Orion does his best to dominate the skyline as he always did.

Our story is the old clash between history and home. Or to put it another way, the immeasurable impossible space that seems to divide the hearth from the quest.

Listen to this.

.   .   .

On a wild night, driven more by weariness than good sense, King Zeus agreed to let his daughter do it differently. She didn't want to get married and sit out some war, while her man, god or not, underwent the ritual metamorphosis from palace prince to craggy hero. She didn't want children. She wanted to hunt. Hunting did her good.

By morning she had packed and set off for her new life in the woods. Soon her fame spread and other women joined her but Artemis didn't care for company. She wanted to be alone. In her solitude she discovered something very odd. She had envied men their long-legged freedom to roam the world and return full of glory to wives who only waited. She knew about the history-makers and the home-makers, the great division that made life possible. Without rejecting it, she had simply hoped to take on the freedoms that belonged to the other side. What if she travelled the world and the seven seas like a hero? Would she find something different or the old things in different disguises?

She found that the whole world could be contained in one place because that place was herself. Nothing had prepared her for this.

The alchemists have a saying: 'Tertium non datur.' The third is not given. That is, the transformation from one element into another, from waste matter into best gold is a mystery, not a formula. No one can predict what will form out of the tensions of opposites and effect a healing change between them. And so it is with the mind that moves from

---

its prison to a free and vast plain without any movement at all. Something new has entered the process. We can only guess.

One evening, when Artemis had lost her quarry, she lit a fire where she was and tried to rest. But the night was shadowy and full of games. She saw herself by the fire; as a child, a woman, a hunter, a Queen. Grabbing the child, she lost sight of the woman, and when she drew her bow, the Queen fled. What would it matter if she crossed the world and hunted down every living creature, as long as her separate selves eluded her? When no one was left she would have to confront herself. Leaving home left nothing behind. It came too, all of it, and waited in the dark. She realised that the only war worth fighting was the one that raged within; the rest were all diversions. In this small space, her hunting miles, she was going to bring herself home. Home was not a place for the faint-hearted; only the very brave could live with themselves.

In the morning she set out and set out every morning day after day.

In her restlessness she found peace.

Then Orion came.

He wandered into Artemis's camp, scattering her dogs and bellowing like a bad actor, his right eye patched and his left arm in a splint. She was a mile away fetching water. When she returned she saw this huge rag of a man eating her goat, raw. When he finished, with a great belch and the fat still fresh around his mouth, he suggested they take a short stroll by the sea's edge. Artemis didn't want that but she was frightened. His reputation hung about him like bad breath.

The ragged shore, rock pitted and dark with weeds, reminded him of his adventures and he recounted them in detail while the tide came in to her waist. There was nowhere he hadn't been, nothing he hadn't seen. He was faster than a hare, stronger than a pair of bulls.

'You smell,' said Artemis, but he didn't hear.

Eventually he allowed her to wade in from the rising water and light a fire for both of them. No, he didn't want her to talk, he knew about her. He had been looking for her. She was a curiosity; he was famous. What a marriage.

But Artemis did talk. She talked about the land she loved and its daily changes. This was where she wanted to stay until she was ready to go. The journey itself was not enough. She spoke quickly, her words hanging on to each other; she had never told anyone before. As she spoke, she knew it was true, and it gave her strength over her fear, to get up and say goodbye. She turned. Orion raped Artemis and fell asleep.

She thought about that time for years. It took a few moments only and she only aware of the hair of his stomach matted with sand, scratching her skin. When he had finished, already snoring, she pushed him off. His snores shook the earth. Later, in the future, the time would remain vivid and unchanged. She wouldn't think of it differently, she wouldn't make it softer or harder. She would just keep it and turn it over in her hands. Her revenge had been swift, simple, and ignominious. She killed him with a scorpion.

In a night, 200,000 years can pass, time moving only in our minds. The steady marking of the seasons, the land well loved and always changing, continues outside, while inside, light years move us on to landscapes that revolve under different skies.

Artemis, lying beside the dead Orion, sees her past changed by a single act. The future is still intact, still unredeemed, but the past is irredeemable. She is not who she thought she was. Every action and decision led her here. The moment had been waiting, the way the top step of the stairs waits for the sleep walker. She had fallen and now she is awake. As she looks at the sky, the sky is peaceful and exciting. A black cloak pinned with silver brooches that never need polish. Somebody lives there, for sure, wrapped up in the glittering folds. Somebody who recognised that the journey by itself is never enough and gave up spaceships long ago in favour of home.

.   .   .

On the beach the waves made pools of darkness around Artemis's feet. She kept the fire burning, warming herself and feeling Orion slowly grow cold. It takes some time for the body to stop playing house.

The fiery circle that surrounded her contained all the clues she needed to recognise that life is for a moment in one shape, then released into another. Monuments and cities would fade away like the people who had built them. No resting place or palace could survive the light years that lay ahead. There was no history that would not be rewritten, and the earliest days were already too far away to see. What would history make of tonight?

Tonight is clear and bright with a cold wind harrying the waves into peaks. The foam leaves slug trails in rough triangles on the sand. The salt smell bristles the air inside her nostrils; her lips are dry. She's thinking about her dogs. They feel like home because she feels like home. The stars show her how to hang in space supported by nothing at all. Without medals or certificates or territories she owns, she can burn as they do, travelling through time until time stops and eternity changes things again. She has noticed that change doesn't hurt her.

It is almost light, which means the disappearing act will soon begin. She wants to lie awake, watching the night fade and the stars fade and the first blue-grey slate of the sky. She wants to see the sun slash the water. But she can't stay awake for everything; some things have to pass her by. So what she doesn't see are the lizards coming out for food or

Orion's eyes turned glassy overnight. A small bird perches on his shoulder, trying to steal a piece of his famous hair.

Artemis waited until the sun was up before she trampled out the fire. She fetched rocks and stones to cover Orion's body from the eagles. She made a high mound that broke the thudding wind as it scored the shore. It was a stormy day, black clouds and a thick orange shining on the horizon. By the time she had finished she was soaked with rain. Her hands were bleeding and her hair kept catching in her mouth. She was hungry but not angry now.

The sand that had been blonde yesterday was now brown with wet. As far as she could see there was grey water white-edged and the birds wheeling above it. Lonely cries, and she was lonely, not for a friend but for a time that had not been violated. The sea was hypnotic. Not the wind or the cold could move her from where she sat like one who waited. She was not waiting; she was remembering. She was trying to find out what had brought her here. The third is not given. All she knew was that she had arrived at the frontiers of common sense and crossed over. She was safe now. No safety without risk and what you risk reveals what you value.

She stood up and in the getting-dark walked away. Not looking behind her but conscious of her feet shaping themselves in the sand. Finally, at the headland, after a bitter climb to where the woods bordered the steep edge, she turned and stared out, seeing the shape of Orion's mound, just visible and her own footsteps walking away. Then it was fully night and she could see nothing to remind her of the night except the stars.

And what of Orion? Dead but not forgotten. For a while he was forced to pass the time in Hades, where he beat up flimsy beasts and cried a lot. Then the gods took pity on him, and drew him up to themselves and placed him in the heavens for all to see. When he rises at dawn, summer is nearly here. When he rises in the evening, beware of winter and storms. If you see him at midnight, it is time to pick the grapes. He keeps his dogs with him, Canis Major and Canis Minor and Sirius, the brightest star in our galaxy. Under his feet, if you care to look, you can see a tiny group of stars: Lepus, the hare, his favourite food.

Orion isn't always at home. Dazzling as he is, like some fighter pilot riding the sky, he glows very faint, if at all, in November. November being the month of Scorpio.

Lives of Saints

That day we saw three Jews in full length black coats and black hats standing on identical stools, looking into the funnel of a pasta machine.

One stepped down from his little stool and went round to the front of the machine where the pasta was stretching out in orange strands. He took two strands and held them up high, so that they dropped against his coat. He looked like he had been decorated with medal ribbon.

They bought the machine. The Italian boys in T-shirts carried it to the truck. The Jews had bought the machine so that they could make pasta like ringlets to sell in their shop. Their shop sold sacred food and the blinds were always half drawn. The floor was just floorboard not polished and the glass counter stood chest high. They served together in their hats and coats. They wrapped things in greaseproof paper. They did this every day except Saturday and when the machine came they made pasta too. They lined the top of the glass counter with wooden trays and they lined the trays with greaseproof paper. Then they laid out the ringlets of fusilli in colours they liked, liking orange best, in memory of the first day. The shop was dark but for the pasta that glowed and sang from the machine.

· · ·

It is true that on bright days we are happy. This is true because the sun on the eyelids effects chemical changes in the body. The sun also diminishes the pupils to pinpricks, letting the light in less. When we can hardly see we are most likely to fall in love. Nothing is commoner in summer than love, and I hesitate to tell you of the commonplace, but I have only one story to tell and this is it.

In the shop where the Jews stood in stone relief, like Shadrach, Meshach and Abednego in the fiery furnace, there was a woman who liked to do her shopping in four ounces.

Even the pasta that fell from the scales in flaming water-falls trickled into her bag. I was always behind her, coming in from the hot streets to the cool dark that hit like a church. What did she do with her tiny parcels laid in lines on the glass top?

Before she paid for them she counted them. If there were not sixteen, she asked for something else, if there were more than sixteen, she had a thing taken away.

I began following her. To begin with I followed just a little way, then, as my obsession increased, I followed in ever greater circles, from the shop to her home, through the park past the hospital. I lost all sense of time and space and sometimes it seemed to me that I was in the desert or the jungle and still following. Sometimes we were aboriginal in our arcane pathways and other times we walked one street.

I say we. She was oblivious of me. To begin with I kept a respectful distance. I walked on the other side of the road.

Then, because she did not notice, I came closer and closer. Close enough to see that she coloured her hair; the shade was not consistent. One day her skirt had a hanging thread and I cut it off without disturbing her. At last, I started to walk beside her. We fell in step without the least difficulty. And still she gave no sign of my presence.

I rummaged through the out-of-print sections in second hand bookshops and spent all my spare time in the library. I learned astronomy and studied mathematics and pored over the drawings of Leonardo da Vinci in order to explain how a watermill worked. I was so impatient to tell her what I had discovered that I began to wait for her outside her house. Eventually I knocked on the door and knocked on the door sharp at 7 a.m. every morning after that. She was always ready. In winter she carried a torch.

After a few months we were spending the whole of the day together. I made sandwiches for our lunch. She never questioned my choice of filling though I noticed she threw away the ones with sardine.

St Teresa of Avila: 'I have no defence against affection. I could be bribed with a sardine.'

So it is for me for whom kindness has always been a surprise.

In the lives of saints I look for confirmation of excess. To them it is not strange to spend nights on a mountain or to forgo food. For them, the visionary and the everyday coincide. Above all, they have no domestic virtues, preferring intensity to comfort. Despite their inhospitable ways, they ferment with unexpected life, like those bleak railway cuttings that host horizontal dandelions. They know there is no passion without pain.

As I told her this, as I had told her so many things, she turned to me and said, 'Sixteen years ago I lived in a hot country with my husband who was important. We had servants and three children. There was a young man who worked for us. I used to watch his body through the window. In the house we lived such clean lives, always washed and talcumed against the sweat. Not the heavy night nor the heat of the day could unsettle us. We knew how to dress.

'One evening, when the boards were creaking under the weather, he came past us, where we sat eating small biscuits and drinking tea, and he dropped two baskets of limes on the floor. He was so tired that he spilt the baskets and went down on his knees under my husband's feet. I looked down and saw my husband's black socks within his black shoes. His toe kicked at a lime. I ducked under the table collecting what I could, and I could smell the young man, smelling of the day and the sun. My husband crossed his legs and I heard him say, "No need for that, Jane."

'Later, when we put out the lamps, and I went to my room and Stephen went to his, my armpits were wet and my face glowed as though I'd been drinking.

'I knew he would come. I took off my nightgown four or five times, wondering how to greet him. It didn't matter. Not then or afterwards. Not any of the two months that followed. My heart swelled. I had a whale's heart. The arteries of a whale's heart are so wide that a child could crawl through. I found I was pregnant.

'On the night I told him, he told me he had to go away. He asked me to go with him and I looked at the verandah and the lamps and Stephen's door that was closed and the children's door that was ajar. I looked at his body. I said I had to stay and he put his head on my stomach and cried.

'On the day he left I lay in my room and when I heard his flight booming over the house, I wrapped my head in a towel. Stephen opened the door and asked, "Are you staying?"

'I told him I was. He said, "Never mention this again."

'I never did. Not that nor anything else.'

We walked on in silence. We walked through the hours of the day until we arrived at nightfall and came to a castle protected by a moat. Lions guarded the gateway.

'I'm going in now,' she said.

I looked up from my thoughts and saw an ordinary house fronted by a pretty garden with a pair of tabby cats washing their paws. Which was the story and which was real? Could it be true that a woman who had not spoken for sixteen years, except to order her food in four ounces, was now walking into this small house full of everyday things? Was it not more likely that she would disappear into her magic kingdom and leave me on the other side of the water, my throat clogged with feelings that resist words?

I followed her across the moat and saw our reflection in the water. I wanted to reach down and scoop her in my arms, let her run over my body until both of us were wet through. I wanted to swim inside her.

We crossed the moat. She fed me on boiled cabbage. I have heard it is a cure for gout. She never spoke as we ate, and afterwards she lit a candle and led me upstairs. I was surprised to see a mosquito net in England.

Time is not constant. Time in stories least of all. Anyone can fall asleep and lose generations in their dreams. The night I spent with her has taken up my whole life and now I live attached to myself like a codicil. It is not because I lack interests; indeed, I have recently reworked Leonardo's drawings and built for myself a fine watermill. It is that being with her allowed me to be myself. There was no burden to live normally. Now I know so many stories and such a collection of strange things that I wonder who would like them since I cannot do them justice on my own. The heart of a whale is the height of a man . . .

. . .

I left her at dawn. The street was quiet, only a cat and the electric whirr of the milk van. I kept looking back at the candle in the window until it was as far away as the faint point of a fading star. In the early sky the stars had faded by the time I reached home. There was the retreating shape of the moon and nothing more.

Every day I went into the shop where the Jews stood in stone relief and I bought things that pleased me. I took my time, time being measured in four ounces. She never came in.

I waited outside her house for some years until a FOR SALE sign appeared and a neighbour told me that the woman next door had vanished. I felt such pleasure then, to know that she was wandering the world, and that one day, one day I might find her again.

When I do, all the stories that are folded into this one can be shaken out and let loose, but until then, like the lives of saints, more is contained than can be revealed. The world itself will roll up like a scroll taking time and space away.

All stories end here.

O'Brien's First Christmas

Anyone who looked up could see it: TWENTY-SEVEN SHOP-PING DAYS TO CHRISTMAS, in red letters, followed by a storm of dancing Santas, then a whirlwind of angels, trumpets rampant.

The department store was very large. If you were to lay its merchandise end to end, starting with a silk stocking and closing on a plastic baby Jesus, you would have belted the world. The opulence of the store defeated all shoppers. Even in the hectic twenty-seven days to Christmas, even including the extended opening hours, there was no exodus of goods that could make the slightest impression on the well stocked shelves.

O'Brien, who worked in the Pet Department, had watched women stacking their baskets with hand and body lotion in an attractive reindeer wrap. Customers who looked quite normal were falling in delight upon pyramids of fondant creams packed in Bethlehem-by-Night boxes. It made no difference. Whatever they demolished returned. This phenomenon, as far as O'Brien could calculate, meant that two-thirds of the spending world would be eating sticky stuff or spreading it over themselves on December 25th.

She poured out a measure of hand and body lotion and broke open a fondant cream. The filling was the same in both. Somewhere, in a town no one visited, stood a factory dedicated to the manufacture of pale yellow sticky stuff waiting to be despatched in labelless vats to profiteers who traded exclusively in Christmas.

O'Brien didn't like Christmas. Every year she prayed for an ordinary miracle to take her away from the swelling round of ageing aunts who knitted her socks and asked about her young man. She didn't have a young man. She lived alone and worked in the Pet Department for company. At a staff discount of 35 percent it made sense for her to have a pet of her own, but her landlady, a Christian Scientist, did not approve of what she called 'Stray Molecules.'

'Hair,' she said, 'carries germs, and what is hairier than an animal?'

So O'Brien faced another Christmas alone.

In the store shoppers enjoyed the kind of solidarity we read about in the war years. There was none of the vulgar pushing and shoving usually associated with peak time buying. People made way for one another in the queues and chatted about the weather and the impending snowfall.

'Snow for Christmas,' said one. 'That's how it should be.' It was right and nice. Enough presents, enough money, clean flame-effect log fires courtesy of the Gas Board. Snow for the children.

O'Brien flicked through the Lonely Hearts. There were extra pages of them at Christmas, just as there was extra everything else. How could it be that column after column of sane, loving, slim men and women, without obvious perversions, were spending Christmas alone? Were the happy families in the department store a beguiling minority?

She had once answered a Lonely Hearts advertisement and eaten dinner with a small young man who mended organ pipes. He had suggested they get married that night by special licence. O'Brien had declined on the grounds that a whirlwind romance would tire her out after so little practice. It seemed rather like going to advanced aerobics when you couldn't manage five minutes on the exercise bicycle. She had asked him why he was in such a hurry.

'I have a heart condition.'

So it was like aerobics after all.

After that she had joined a camera club, where a number of men had been keen to help her in the darkroom, but all of them had square hairy hands that reminded her of joke shop gorilla paws.

'Don't set your sights too high,' her aunts warned.

But she did. She set them in the constellations, in the roaring lion, and the flanks of the bull. In December, when the stars were bright, she saw herself in another life, happy.

'You've got to have a dream,' she told the Newfoundland pup destined to become a Christmas present. 'I don't know what I want. I'm just drifting.'

She'd heard that men knew what they wanted, so she asked Clive, the Floor Manager.

'I'd like to run my own branch of McDonald's. A really big one with full breakfasts and party seating.'

O'Brien tried, but she couldn't get excited. It was the same with vacuum cleaners; she could use the power but where was the glamour?

When she returned to her lodgings that evening her landlady was solemnly nailing a holly wreath to the front door.

'This is not for myself, you understand, it is for my tenants. Next I will hang paper chains in the hall.' O'Brien's landlady always spoke very slowly because she had been a Hungarian Countess. A Countess does not rush her words.

O'Brien, still in her red duffle coat, found herself holding on to one end of a paper chain, while her landlady creaked up the aluminium steps, six tacks between her teeth.

'Soon be Christmas,' said O'Brien. 'I'm making a New Year's resolution to change my life, otherwise, what's the point?'

'Life has no point,' said her landlady. 'You would be better to get married or start an evening class. For the last seven years I have busied myself with brass rubbings.'

The hall was cold. The paper chain was too short. O'Brien didn't want advice. She made her excuses and mounted the stairs. Her landlady, perhaps stung by a pang of sympathy, offered her a can of sardines for supper.

'They are not in tomato sauce but olive oil.'

O'Brien though, had other plans.

· · ·

Inside her room she began to make a list of the things people thought of as their future: Marriage, children, a career, travel, a home, enough money, lots of money. Christmas time brought these things sharply into focus. If you had them, any of them, you could feel especially pleased with life over the twelve days of feasting and family. If you didn't have them, you felt the lack more keenly. You felt like an outsider. Odd that a festival to celebrate the most austere of births should become the season of conspicuous consumption. O'Brien didn't know much about theology but she knew there had been a muck-up somewhere.

As she looked at the list, she began to realise that an off the peg future, however nicely designed, wouldn't be the life she sensed when she looked up at the stars. Immediately she felt guilty. Who was she to imagine she could find something better than other people's best?

'What's wrong with settling down and getting married?' she said out loud.

'Nothing,' said her landlady, appearing around the door without knocking. 'It's normal. We should all try to be normal,' and she put down the sardines on O'Brien's kitchenette, and left.

'Nothing wrong,' thought O'Brien, 'but what is right for me?'

· · ·

She lay awake through the night, listening to the radio beaming out songs and bonhomie for Christmas. She wanted to stay under the blankets forever, being warm and watching the bar of the electric fire. She remembered a story she had read as a child about a princess invited to a ball. Her father offered her more than two hundred gowns to choose from but none of them fitted and they were too difficult to alter. At last she went in her silk shift with her hair down, and still she was more beautiful than anyone.

'Be yourself,' said O'Brien, not altogether sure what she meant.

At the still point of the night O'Brien awoke with a sense that she was no longer alone in the room. She was right. At the bottom of her bed sat a young woman wearing an organza tutu.

O'Brien didn't bother to panic. She was used to her neighbour's friends blundering into the wrong room.

'Vicky is next door,' she said. 'Do you want the light on?'

'I'm the Christmas fairy,' said the woman. 'Do you want to make a wish?'

'Come on,' said O'Brien, realising her visitor must be drunk. 'I'll show you the way.'

'I'm not going anywhere,' said the woman. 'This is the address I was given. Do you want love or adventure or what? We don't do money.'

O'Brien thought for a moment. Perhaps this was a new kind of singing telegram. She decided to play along, hoping to discover the sender.

'What can you offer?'

The stranger pulled out a photograph album. 'In here are all the eligible men in London. It's indexed, so if you want one with a moustache, look under "M," where you will also find "moles." '

O'Brien had a look. She could think of nothing but those booklets of Sunny Smiles she used to buy to help the orphans. Seeing her lack of enthusiasm, the stranger offered her a second album.

'Here's one with all the eligible women. It's all the same to me.'

'Shouldn't you be singing all this?' asked O'Brien, thinking it was time to change the subject.

'Why?' said the fairy. 'Does conversation bother you?'

'No, but you are a Singing Telegram.'

'I am not a Singing Telegram. I am a fairy. Now what is your wish?'

'OK,' said O'Brien, wanting to go back to sleep. 'I wish I was blonde.'

Then she must have gone back to sleep straightaway, because the next thing she heard was the alarm ringing in her ears. She dozed, she was late, no time for anything, just into her red duffle coat and out into a street full of shoppers, mindful of their too few days to go.

· · ·

At work, on her way up to the Pet Department, she met Janice from Lingerie, who said, 'Your hair's fantastic. I didn't recognise you at first.'

O'Brien was confused. She hadn't had time to brush her hair. Was it standing on end? She went into the Ladies and peered into the mirror. She was blonde.

'It really suits you,' said Kathleen, from Fabrics and Furnishings. 'You should do more with your make-up now.'

'Do more?' thought O'Brien, who did nothing. She decided to go back home, but in the lift on the way out, she met the actor who had come to play Santa . . .

'It's awful in the Grotto. It's made of polystyrene and everyone knows that's bad for the lungs.' O'Brien sympathised.

'Listen,' said Santa, 'there's two dozen inflatable gnomes in the basement. I've got to blow them up. If you'll help me, I'll buy you lunch.'

For the first time in her life O'Brien abandoned herself to chaos and decided it didn't matter. What surprises could remain for a woman who had been visited in the night by a Non-Singing Telegram and subsequently turned blonde? Blowing up gnomes was a breath of fresh air.

'I like your hair,' said the actor Santa.

'Thanks,' said O'Brien, 'I've only just had it done.'

· · ·

At the vegetarian cafe where every lentil bake came with its own sprig of holly, Santa asked O'Brien if she would like to come for Christmas dinner.

'There won't be any roast corpse though.'

'That's all right,' said O'Brien, 'I'm not a vegetarian but I don't eat meat.'

'Then you are a vegetarian.'

'Aren't you supposed to join something?'

'No,' said Santa. 'Just be yourself.'

In the mirror on the wall O'Brien smiled. She was starting to like being herself. She didn't go back to work that afternoon. She went shopping like everybody else. She bought new clothes, lots of food, and a set of fairy lights. When the man at the stall offered her a cut price Christmas tree, she shouldered it home. Her landlady saw her arriving.

'You are early today,' she said very slowly. 'I see you are going to get pine needles on my carpet.'

'Thanks for the sardines,' said O'Brien. 'Have a bag of satsumas.'

'Your hair is not what it was last night. Did something happen to you?'

'Yes,' said O'Brien, 'but it's a secret.'

'I hope it was not a man.'

'No it was a woman.'

Her landlady paused, and said, 'I am going now to listen to the Gospel according to St Luke on my wireless.'

·   ·   ·

O'Brien put the potatoes in the oven and strung her window with fairy lights. Outside the sky was strung with stars.

At eight o'clock, when Santa arrived, wet and cold and still in uniform, O'Brien lit the candles beneath the tree. She said,

'If you could make a wish what would it be?'

'I'd wish to be here with you.'

'Even if I wasn't blonde?'

'Even if you were bald.'

'Merry Christmas,' said O'Brien.

The World and Other Places

When I was a boy I made model aeroplanes.

We never had the money to go anywhere, sometimes we didn't have the money to go to the shop. There were six of us at night in the living room, six people and six carpet tiles. Usually the tiles were laid two by three in a dismal rectangle, but on Saturday night, aeroplane night, we took one each and sat cross legged with the expectation of an Arabian prince. We were going to fly away, and we held on to the greasy underside of our mats, waiting for the magic word to lift us.

Bombay, Cairo, Paris, New York. We took it in turns to say the word, and the one whose word it was, took my model aeroplane and spun it where it hung from the ceiling, round and round our blow-up globe. We had saved cereal tokens for the globe and it had been punctured twice. Iceland was held together by Sellotape and Great Britain was only a rubber bicycle patch on the panoply of the world.

I had memorised the flight times from London Heathrow to anywhere you could guess at in the world. It was my job to announce our flying time, the aircraft data, and to wish the passengers a comfortable trip. I pointed out landmarks on the way and we would lean over the fireplace to take a look at Mont Blanc or crane our necks round the back of the settee to get a glimpse of the Rockies.

Half way through our trip, Mother, who was Chief Steward, swayed down the aisle with cups of tea and toast and Marmite. After that, Dad came forward with next week's jobs around the house scribbled on little bits of paper. We dipped into the pouch, and somebody, the lucky one, would get Duty Free on theirs, and they didn't have to do a thing.

When we reached our destination, we were glad to stand up and stretch our legs. Then my sister gave us each a blindfold. We put it on, and sat quietly, dreaming, imagining, while one of us started talking about the strange place we were visiting.

How hot it is getting off the plane. Hot and stale like opening the door of a tumble drier. There are no lights to show us where to go. Death will be this way; a rough passage with people we have never met and a hasty run across the tarmac to the terminal building.

Inside, in the day-for-night illumination, a group of Indians were playing cellos. Who are these orchestral refugees? Can it be part of the service? Beyond them, urchins with bare feet are leaping up and down with ragged cardboard signs, each bearing the name of someone more important than ourselves. These are the people who will be whisked away in closed cars to comfortable beds. The rest of us will search for the bus.

Luggage. Heaven or Hell in the hereafter will be luggage or the lack of it. The ones who recognised that love is enough and that possessions are borrowed pastimes, will float free through the exit sign, their arms ready to hug their friends, their toothbrush in their pocket. The ones who stayed up late, gathering and gathering like demented bees, will find that you can take it with you. The joke is that you have to carry it yourself.

Here comes the bus. It has three wheels, maybe four, and the only part noisier than the engine is the horn. All human life is here. I am travelling between a chicken coop and a fortune teller. The chickens peck at my legs and suddenly the fortune teller grabs my palm. She laughs in my face.

'When you grow up you will learn to fly.'

For the rest of the journey I am bitten by mosquitoes.

At last we have reached the Hotel Cockroach. Dusty mats cover the mud floor and the Reception Clerk has an open wound in his cheek. He tells me he was stabbed but not to worry. Then he serves me lukewarm tea and shows me my room. It has a view over the incinerator and is farthest from the bathroom. At least I will not learn to think highly of myself.

In the darkness and the silence I can hear, far below, the matter of life continuing without me. The night-shift. What are they doing, these people who come and go, cleaning, bringing food, wanting money, wanting to fight. What will they eat? Where will they sleep? Do they love someone? How many of them will see morning? Will I?

Dreams. The smell of incense and frangipani. The moon sailing on her back makes white passages on the dun floor. The moon and the white clouds at the window. How many times have I seen it? How many times do I stop and look as if I had never seen it before? Perhaps it is true that the world is made new again every day but our minds are not. The clamp that holds me will not let me go.

During the night a mouse gave birth behind the skirting board.

At the end of my story, my family and I swopped anecdotes and exchanged souvenirs. Later, we retired to bed with the weariness of a traveller's reunion. We had done what the astronauts do, travelled in space that did not belong to us, uncoupled ourselves from time.

That night, I knew I would get away, better myself. Not because I despised who I was, but because I did not know who I was. I was waiting to be invented. I was waiting to invent myself.

. . .

The pilot and I went up in the aeroplane. It was a Cessna, modern and beautiful, off white with a blue stripe right round it and a nose as finely balanced as a pedigree muzzle. I wanted to cup it in both hands and say, 'Well done boy.'

In spite of the air conditioned cockpit, overwarm and muzzy in an unexpected economy class way, the pilot had a battered flying jacket stuffed behind his seat. It was authentic, grubby sheepskin and a steel zip. I asked him why he needed it.

'Romance,' he said, grinning. 'Flying is romantic, even now, even so.'

We were under a 747 at the time, and I thought of the orange seats crammed three abreast on either side, and all the odds and ends of families struggling with their plastic trays and beach gear.

'Is that romantic?' I said, pointing upwards.

He glanced out of the reinforced glass.

'That's not flying. That's following the road.'

For a while we travelled in silence. I watched him; strong jaw with necessary stubble. Brown eyes that never left the sky. He was pretending to be the only man in the air. His dream was the first dream, when men in plus fours and motorcycle goggles pedalled with the single mindedness of a circus chimp to get their wooden frames and canvas wings upwards and upwards and upwards. It was a solo experience even when there were two of you.

What did Amy Johnson say? 'If the whole world were flying beside me I would still be flying alone.' Rhetoric, you think, frontier talk. Then you reach your own frontier and it's not rhetoric anymore.

My parents were so proud of me when I joined the Air Force. I stood in our cluttered living room in my new uniform and I felt like an angel on a visit. I felt like Gabriel come to tell the shepherds the Good News.

'Soon you'll have your own wings,' said my mother.

My father had bought a bottle of Scotch.

In my bedroom, the model aeroplanes had been carefully dusted. Sopwith Camel. Spitfire. Tiger Moth. I picked them up one by one and turned over their balsa wood frames and rice paper wings. I never used a kit. What hopes they carried. More than the altar at church. More than a good school report. In the secret places, under the fuselage, stuck to the tail-fin, I had hidden my hopes.

My mother came in. 'Will you take them with you?' I shook my head. I'd be laughed at, made fun of. Yet each of us in our bunks at lights-out would be thinking of model aeroplanes and the things from home we couldn't talk about anymore.

She said, 'I gave them a wipe anyway.'

. . .

Bombay. Cairo. Paris. New York. I've been to those places now. The curious thing is that no matter how different they are, the people are all preoccupied with the same things, that is, the same thing; how to live. We have to eat, we want to make money, but in every pause the question returns: How shall I live?

I saw three things that made this clear to me.

The first was a beggar in New York. He was sitting, feet apart, head in hands, on a low wall beside a garage. As I walked by him, he whispered, 'Do you have two dollars?' I gave him the folded bills, and he said, 'Can you sit with me a minute?'

His name was Tony. He was a compulsive gambler trying to go straight. He thought he might land a job on Monday morning if only he could sleep the weekend in a hostel, get some rest, be clean. For a week he had been sleeping by the steam duct of the garage.

I gave him the hostel money and a little more for food and the clenched fist of his body unfolded. He was talkative, gentle. Already in his mind he had the job, was making a go of it, and had met a sweet woman in a snack bar. Was that the gambler in him or ordinary human hope? Already in his mind he was looking past the job and the apartment into the space that had turned him over the wall.

'Nobody used to look at me,' he said. 'Even when I had

money, I was one of those guys who get looked through. It's like being a ghost. If no one can see you you're dead. What's the point of trying to live if you are already dead?'

He shook my hand and thanked me. He was going to the hostel before it closed, or maybe he was going to a dog. I can't know. I don't need to know. There's enough I need to know just for myself.

I said there were three things. The second was a dress designer living over her studio in Milan. She was rich, she was important. She liked airmen. I used to sit with her in the studio, she never had time for a meal or a trip somewhere, she ate like an urchin, one leg hooked round her stool, palm full of olives. She spat the stones at her models. We were talking one night and she got angry. She prodded me with the shears she kept on her work table.

'Stop thinking,' she said. 'The more you think, the faster you cut your own throat. What is there to think about? It always ends up the same way. In your mind there is a bolted door. You have to work hard not to go near that door. Parties, lovers, career, charity, babies, who cares what it is, so long as you avoid the door. There are times, when I am on my own, fixing a drink, walking upstairs, when I see the door waiting for me. I have to stop myself pulling the bolt and turning the handle. Why? On the other side of the door is a mirror, and I will have to see myself. I'm not afraid of what I am. I'm afraid I will see what I am not.'

. . .

I said there were three things. The third was a woman in the park with her dog. The dog was young. The woman was old. Every so often she took out a bottle of water and a little bowl and gave the dog a drink.

'Come on Sandy,' she'd say, when he'd finished, and they would both disappear into the bushes, the dog's tail bobbing behind.

She was poor, I could see that. Put us side by side and how do we look? I'm six feet tall in a smart airman's uniform and I have a strong grip and steady eyes. She's about five feet high and threadbare. I could lift her with one hand.

But when she met my gaze one day I dropped my eyes and blushed like a teenager. I was walking past her in the opposite direction and I smiled and said, 'How are you?'

She looked at me with eyes that have long since pierced through the cloud cover and as we talked, I realised she was happy. Happy. The kind of happiness that comes from a steadiness inside. This was genuine. This was not someone who had turned away from the bolted door. It was open. She was on the other side.

For some years, early in my Air Force days, I did not bother myself with the single simple question that is the hardest in the world. How shall I live? I was living wasn't I? I was adventure, manliness, action. That's how we define ourselves isn't it?

Then one day I awoke with the curious sensation of no longer being myself. I hadn't turned into a beetle or a werewolf and my friends treated me in the same way as before. I put on my favourite well-worn clothes, bought newspapers, took a holiday, went to Milan, walked in the park. At last I called on the doctor.

'Doctor I'm not myself anymore.'

He asked me about my sex life and prescribed a course of antidepressants.

I went to the library and borrowed books from the philosophy and psychology sections, terrified in case I should be spotted by someone who knew me. I read Jung who urged me to make myself whole. I read Lacan who wants me to accept that I'm not.

None of it helped me. All the time I thought crazily, 'If this isn't me then I must be somewhere else.'

That's when I started travelling so much, left the forces, bought my own plane. Mostly I teach flying now, and sometimes I take out families who have won the First Prize in a packet soup competition. It doesn't matter. I have plenty of free time and I do what I need to do, which is to look for myself.

I know that if I fly for long enough, for wide enough, for

far enough, I'll catch a signal on the radar that tells me there's another aircraft on my wing. I'll glance out of the reinforced glass, and it won't be a friendly pilot that I'll see, all stubble and brown eyes. It will be me. Me in the cockpit of that other plane.

I went home to visit my mother and father. I flew over their village, taxied down their road and left the nose of my plane pushed up against the front door. The tail was just on the pavement and I was worried that some traffic warden might issue a ticket for obstruction, so I hung a sign on the back that said 'FLYING DOCTOR.'

I'm always nervous about going home, just as I am nervous about rereading books that have meant a lot to me.

My parents wanted me to tell them about the places I've been and what I've seen, their eyes were eager and full of life.

Bombay. Cairo. Paris. New York. We have invented them so many times that to tell the truth will be a disappointment. The blow-up globe still hangs over the mantelpiece, its plastic crinkly and torn. The countries of the Common Market are held together with red tape.

We went through my postcards one by one. I gave them presents; a sari for my mother and a Stetson for my father. They are the children now.

Time passes through the clock. It's time for me to leave. They come outside to wave me off.

'It's a lovely plane,' says my mother. 'Does it give you much trouble?'

I rev the engine and the neighbours stand in astonishment in their doorways as the plane gathers speed down our quiet road. A moment before the muzzle breaks through the apostal window in the church, I take off, rising higher and higher, and disappearing into the end stream of the sun.

Disappearance I

This morning I noticed there was one room missing.

I had woken up as usual to the morning noise of singing drills and chirpy workmen, and the aviary of tradesmen building individual nests out of the hollow of a derelict house.

I wound up my clockwork sufficiently to tick out onto the waking streets and buzz a newspaper off the sleep-deprived vendor. Like the rest of the poor in sleep of the coming twenty-first century he was a money junkie, trading shut-eye for a tight fist. Nobody can afford to sleep any-more. Do you realise how much it costs?

'Wake-up Benny,' I said, his head on a pillow of tabloid tits.

'Where's the money?' he said. 'Give me the money.' Then, as the morning light took a swing at his retina, he saw it was me, and slumped back again onto the newsprint bosoms.

'You need to get some sleep,' I said.

'Some of us have got a wife and kids to support.'

'And a Mercedes and a mistress.'

He scowled at me through the slits above his nose.

'Get lost.'

'I will, I'm going back to bed.'

'Bloody pervert.'

. . .

I know, I know. It's the likes of me who . . .

The likes of me who what? I am single. I have a girl-friend. I rent a nice flat with a kitchen, a sitting room and a bedroom, and in the bedroom, with the curtains drawn, sometimes open, sometimes in the middle of the day, some-times for pleasurable hours all morning, naked, warm, I sleep.

How did it start?

It started before I was born. The little kicking foot pitch-ing in the goal-space of my mother's belly. The round ball of me netted and home, safe to sleep before the long header down the tunnel and out into a stadium of lights.

When I was born. Pharaoh-domed and blue. Pointed and Picasso'd. A Cubist baby of lines and planes. Not breathing human yet. Still corded to God's architecture. Small gasps and liquid eyes. Look at me now, here I am, I slept.

When I was a wriggler, a crawler, a toddler, an upright, a walker, a runner, a high-flyer, spaced-out, I slept. It came naturally to me. I lay down, closed my eyes. I slept.

Everyone I knew slept too. Even my parents. The Vicar. And then.

. . .

And then I was offered the job of a particle in factory physics. I was offered the job of an electron in an office atom. I was offered the job of a frequency for a radio station. People told me I could easily make it as a ray in a ray gun. What's the matter with you, don't you want to do well? I wanted to be a beach bum and work on my wave function. I have always loved the sea.

Most of the jobs advertised these days insist on a non-sleeper. Sleeping is dirty, unhygienic, wasteful and disrespectful to others. All public spaces are designated 'Non-Sleeping' and even a quick nap on a park bench carries a £50 fine. You can still sleep in your own home but all new beds are required by law to have a personal alarm clock built into the mattress. If you get caught on a bed-check with a dead alarm, that's another £50 fine. Three fines and you are disqualified from sleeping for a year.

I don't have a new bed. When I invited my girlfriend to my flat for the first time, she had never seen a bed like mine.

'Wow. Is that an antique?'

'Do you like antiques?'

'Well, they're so . . . old.'

'This is my bed. My one and only.'

'What do you use it for?'

'I sleep in it.'

'For special occasions?'

'Every night. Nine or ten hours every night.'

'You mean every week.'

I took her in my arms. Tonight, this night, tomorrow night, the nights in gentle stars, with you, if you like, rolled and dark and quilted with stars. I asked her to sleep with me.

'You mean lie awake with you? Everybody wants to know if we're lying awake together.'

'Sleeping together.'

She was worried. Now she knew she was with a real heavy number.

'Nine or ten hours a night?'

I nodded, addicted, dumb, sleep-hooked, sleepy.

She left. I advertised in an underground magazine called *SNOOZE*. 'Girlfriend wanted. Must have own bed.'

I am not rich but my sister is. Lie her down and cover her in gold and not even her left eye would be showing. She works for a German giant called Fafner UK. Their business is other people's money and the more they have the more they want. My sister was one of the first to give up sleep for the sake of her career. She works a twenty-hour day in two time zones. She worries about me.

. . .

'Hello. It's your sister.'

   'It's the middle of the night.'

   'I was worried about you.'

   'Don't worry about me.'

   'I saw your small ad in *SNOOZE* magazine.'

   'How did you know it was me?'

   'You put your name, address and phone number.'

She told me to see a doctor and get some waking pills. She offered me a job. I asked her why she had been reading *SNOOZE* magazine. She didn't like that. She knows it's pornography. If you can find it in a shop it's always the top shelf, and by top shelf I mean you have to ask the assistant for a ladder. It takes a particular kind of somnolent courage to clatter the aluminium steps through the eager beavers in the Hobbies Section and clamber up past Adult Entertainment, S-M, Snuff, Corpse, until you can fumble for the plain brown wrapper of *SNOOZE*. I have asked the assistant to keep it under the counter for me, the way she does with the incest magazine, *MOTHERFUCKER*. She shook her head. 'I can't do that with *SNOOZE*. Not *SNOOZE*. In any case, from next month you'll have to sign for it.'

So there I was, with a Sleep magazine on prescription. Yes, prescription. Doctor's orders dear Sister. It's my new job, didn't I tell you about that?

· · ·

I know we are walking home by a roundabout route, but after I bought my paper this morning I decided to go to the park and feed the rubber ducks. The real ducks died because so many people were feeding them in the new twenty-four-hour working day that not a drake nor a duck had a moment to itself. Some sank under the weight of soggy bread, others exploded. The rubber variety are much more adaptable.

The sun shone. Maddeningly, it won't shine during the night, but we are working on it.

I walked quickly, purposefully through the dead-eyed crowds taking a breakfast break, until I got clear of the feeding areas and on to a crisp grass knoll. No one ever comes up here, it's too aimless, there's no reason to come up here, no swings, no cafe, not even a bench.

I flung myself down and watched the clouds bumping each other, the break and mend of a morning sky. My body was relaxed and the ordered chords of my thinking mind began to separate into component notes, to replay themselves without effort, without purpose, trailing into . . . sleep.

I dreamed I was a single moment in a single day.

A note struck and vanished. A sounding. A reckoning. Gone.

I was awoken rudely. Far too rudely. The keeper prodded

me with a sharp stick as though I were a beast in a zoo. I opened my eyes and the clouds were gone. A grey face, a dirty uniform, the customary slashes of the barely open lids, and the clenched fist scrawling a ticket.

Do you remember when park keepers used to spear litter and chat to mothers at the sand pit? No more. These scabrous patrols have stun batons and two-way radios. They clean up homosexuals and sleepers and prefer to be known by their offical tag of Public Space Enforcement Officers.

Unfortunately mine had fallen over. It happened suddenly. He was punching out his fine code when he toppled forward, face down into the grass. I turned him over and felt his pulse. Now I would be charged with murder.

He was not dead. He was snoring.

Carefully, I put his hat over his eyes and made a little palisade around him out of the plastic spokes and fluttery tape the keepers carry to cordon off areas of maximum security, like the rubber duck pond.

As I went down the knoll I looked back. There was a faint blue gas settling at his head. I'd heard of this but I'd never seen it. It's what happens when the dreams return.

Which is what I am. A dreamer. I should write that with a capital, it has a title, it exists. Someone has to do it. I don't know how many of us there are. My ID card says Civil Servant and I try to dream as politely as possible.

I dream because you don't. Dreaming is my job and my dreams are tele-electronically recorded and transmitted at Dream-points around the City.

When the no-sleep lifestyle was pioneered, it was soon discovered that people functioned better if they had a dream-boost. A pad on the heart and the wrist can electronically lull the body into a sleep state in seconds, but it can't dream. I can, and if you'd like to try me, last night's will be on the headset in about an hour.

'You're working as a Dreamer?'

'Yes, and you're ringing me in the middle of the night.'

'I'm sorry. I'm so sorry. I had no idea you were official.'

'Shall I send you a free disc?'

'Oh I'd love that. Mark it private will you?'

She put down the phone. Tough girls don't dream.

Mark it private. The same could be said of the Sleep Bar I go to at the weekends. It's called Morpheus's Cave. It's dark, silent, racked with beds and open arms. I was hoping to find a girlfriend there, groping round with a torch, looking for a nice face. The trouble is, it's difficult to know how we'd get on when she is awake.

Tonight I'm trying the Sleeping Beauty. It caters for a younger crowd who just want to drop off for an hour if they're passing. Maybe I'll find someone to talk to. Talking and dreaming. Dreaming and talking. All these clocks and no time.

In my city of dreams the roads lead nowhere; that is, they lead off the edge of the world into infinite space. Under my feet the road quickens, like a moving track at the airport. It is the road itself that carries me forward, until there is nothing under my feet but air. Where to now, without tarmac and map? What direction do I take now that all directions can be taken?

I dream I am in a square with tall houses on three sides. On the fourth side, the house fronts are a facade, and behind them are the pipes and vents and chambers of the underground railway.

I want to get down to the railway. I can hear the noises of the trains and the voices of the stokers. The only way down is by a shaft-ladder covered by a glass manhole. I can't prise the manhole up. I could smash it but I know that I mustn't. A woman comes out from one of the tall houses and asks me to go away. I tell her about the railway and she says it's disused. The builders will be coming in tomorrow.

When she has gone I am in utter despair. How will I ever get down the ladder if the chamber is built over? I find myself scurrying over disused ground, on all fours like an animal, looking for an animal hole to take me away from the topmost world.

These dreams of mine are carefully screened for disruptive elements. Only here, only now, what is between us is true. You and I, this honesty we make.

Sleep with me.

At the Sleeping Beauty I ordered a shot of brandy with a jug of hot milk in it and went to lie down in the Pillow Room. The Pillow Room is where most of the girls go. It's dark, soft, and there's a Dream Screen on the wall. When I walked in they were playing one of my dreams.

'That isn't how it ends,' I said, before I could stop myself. 'It was a nightmare. I wasn't running happily over the just planted earth. I was an animal on derelict ground.'

A couple of girls got up and went off to the ZZZ Bar. I was left alone with a wide-awake redhead squirreling out the contents of her handbag.

She offered me a sleeping pill. I shook my head.

'It's not sleep I need,' I said.

She looked disappointed and lay back on the pillows watching the screen. The dream was over, we were in an advertising break, something about quality of life on a new breakfast cereal called Go!

I rolled over beside her and kissed her surprised mouth. Horizontal contact is strictly forbidden in play-at-it bars like Sleeping Beauty. I moved across a bolster to hide us and let her undo my belt.

Later that night, walking home arm in arm we talked about opening a fish restaurant by the sea. Holiday resorts are Sleep Designated Areas. The only difficulty is that everyone there is too exhausted to eat. Most go intravenous for a fortnight in August.

'I'm lucky,' I said. 'I'm a Dreamer.'

I don't know if she understood. Then came the tough question. The question I had been afraid to ask.

'Will you sleep with me?'

Under the night rug, the star rug, moon as lantern, man in the moon watching over us, dog star at his heels, we lay.

The planets are bodies in the solar system and so are we. You and I in elliptical orbs circling life. It is life we want, but we daren't come too close for fear it might burn us away, this life in its intensity. We call it life force, and it is, force enough to push the shoot through clay. Force enough to impel the baby out of nothing into light.

When I hold you in this night-soaked bed it is courage for the day I seek. Courage that when the light comes I will turn towards it. It couldn't be simpler. It couldn't be harder.

In this little night-covered world with you, I hope to find what I long for; a clue, a map, a bird flying south, and when the light comes we will get dressed together and go.

Head to head, she and I, ordinary receivers of dreams. But the dreams are not ordinary. The coded lunar language is only half heard. The Aztecs believed that the moon would tell the way to the sun god. The way of darkness to the way of light. Sign into speech.

Will it be so? Let me sleep with you. Let me hear the things you cannot say.

And so it was morning and I went to buy the paper. I came back to my flat and went into the kitchen to make coffee. I took a cup to the bedroom and that is when I discovered that the bedroom was no longer there.

I called your name and there was no answer. I stared at the wall, the wall where the door had been, where the bedroom had been.

There was a noise behind me. It was my landlord.

'What are you doing here?' I said.

'Supervising the conversion,' he said. 'Didn't you get my letter?'

He was holding it in his hand. I read it. It informed me that my bedroom was to be made into a separate flat. My bedroom was surplus to requirements. It was quaint, out of date, something like a vegetable allotment in the age of the supermarket. It was a luxury. I couldn't afford it.

'But this is a one-bedroom apartment.'

'You have a kitchen and a sitting room. What more do you want?'

'I want a bedroom.'

He shook his head, in regret, in disbelief, offended. I followed him outside to where a couple of men were fitting a new front door into what had been my wardrobe space. There was a large box on the pavement, marked 'Clothes.'

'Where's my bed?'

'Don't need a bed if you ain't got a bedroom,' said one of the workmen logically.

'Where is it, and where is what was in it?'

There was a leer, or a sneer, or a jeer. They shrugged.

'Ask in The Macbeth,' they said, pointing to the pub at the end of the road.

I ran down there. The Macbeth is a twenty-four-hour swill bar, a thug trough, a beer urinal. As I crashed through the doors into the pounding fists of the bass speakers, I saw my bed, trussed, trophied, pissed on, stabbed, empty.

'Where is she?'

. . .

Sometimes I think I'll find her, as though I had never lost her. Sometimes at the draw and ebb of the sea on a clear night, I see her walking just in front of me and I swear there are footprints. She was a clue I tried to follow but I live in a world that has lost the plot. Sleep now and hope to dream.

Disappearance II

This morning I noticed there was one room missing.

In a house like mine rooms can go missing; we close up entire wings during the winter and the house does not fly at all, but sits among the trees, brooding.

In summer, alight with parties and ablaze with sun, the house is lofty, all movement and voices, hardly a thing of stone at all.

Nevertheless, it is my house in winter that I love, my house clipped and silent, and me its master.

You will understand that I do not trouble myself with covering up the furniture or shutting up the fireplaces. Others do that. Room by room the house is quieted for the winter, until only I am its beating heart. Only I, the rise and fall of its lungs, the house and I breathing together in the night.

It was my father's house, and his father's before him, and so on, back through history as though history were a family album. I flick through a few hundred years and come to myself, gene descended, different from the Archbishop, the Admiral, the Viceroy of India, by my clothes not my face.

My face could be theirs, it is theirs, just as this house was theirs and now is mine.

It is not necessary to prolong life; life prolongs itself. The pen they put down I pick up. The wine they bought I drink. Whose hand turns the knob? Theirs or mine?

When I walk past the family vault and glance at the shelf reserved for me, can I be sure that I do not lie there already? The line between life and death is a couple of inches at most. The width of a door that connects two rooms. The dead are, as we say, on the other side. Indeed they are, the other side of the door, and sometimes the door is open; their hand on the knob or mine?

My family have not been lucky in love. There is a strain of madness on the female side that has been cargoed in the DNA ever since 1590, when the wife of the Admiral had to be locked in the poop of the *Goodship* for six weeks for her own safety. Conditions were not of the best and she starved to death. It is not abnormal for a person to go blind before they die of starvation. They found her, filthy, crawling, dark, and so she is, still, holed down inside us, waiting to break out.

We choose carefully, but the more carefully we choose the more vicious is our disappointment. My mother, as healthy and clean a creature as you could wish for, developed an eating disorder and preferred to take her meals in the stable with the horses. Eventually, to help her, my father let her have her own stall and she slept on straw and ate out of a leather bucket. He had a little saddle made for her so that we children could ride on her back. He called her filly and beauty and treated her as kindly as he could but she had a wild thing's nature and what should have been soft was hoof. My sister and I grew up with a governess, who is here in the house now, using the rooms like tunnels, blinking her way against the light.

I am never sure how many servants we have, a house full or none at all. Things are done but by whom? As I walk from room to room the door I did not enter shuts softly, the fire is lit or swept, there is a tray of refreshments, but no one, no one to say 'Thank you Sir' or curtsey, as in my father's day. In the summer it is quite different. We hire staff like everyone else with a large house open to the public.

But this is not summer. This is winter. The house does not enjoy being violated.

When there was money, real money, the doors were inlaid with mother of pearl and the box hedges were topiary swags. It was my great-grandfather who made a second fortune out of Public Hygiene. That is, he dug the London sewers. I have a sepia photograph of him in his frock coat and top hat standing beside the great blind digging machine on the banks of the Thames.

That sewer, the deepest and biggest of its kind then, silted up within nine months. It had to be abandoned. There it is now, secret, hidden, a history trap. The accumulated waste of the past not dispersed and made neutral by the flow of time, but packed and waiting. Waiting for what? Human greed to bury its face in filth. You see, the sewer served some of the most expensive addresses in London. Early plumbing was a child's affair, without the bends, traps, waste filters, vents, graded outlets, that quietly and efficiently chug away your deposits and mine. Think of straight simple pipes of clay and copper passing from the basin, where Lady Muck bends her head, into the deep sewer. Her diamond earring falls off, down, down into the patient dirt. Think of coins, rings, collar studs in silver, neck pins in gold. Think of teaspoons, medals, watch chains, the boot boy cleaning the boot hooks. Down, down, all down, with the remains of the Clos de Vougeot and the housemaid's swill.

This house has its own private sewer system. I live above a minotaur's maze of brown passages and green chambers. We light our cellars with methane gas piped directly from our ancestral mass. There is a faint smell, not unpleasant, but marked. It amuses me to find my way guided by the last gasp of a good dinner.

There is talk in the village that there is more in these sewers than sewerage. Yes, I say, Yes. But not only these sewers. There is more in your heart than can be spoken. More in your eyes than you will tell. More in the mind of you than anyone can know. More in the night than darkness. More in the river than can be dredged. What more? The hate, envy, malice, greed, stupidity and evil that lie under the floor of everything.

If I have secrets so do you.

My secret life. Secrets scurrying behind the walls like mice in the wainscotting. At night the noises are louder. I have noticed how much talk there is of openness these days which must mean there is a great deal more to hide.

When I open my house to the public I shut away the precious things. The private apartments are locked. My visitors trail their way through an impassive sanitised game of a house playing hide and seek with itself. When I welcome the paying herds at the main door I wear a suit I never wear for any other purpose. It is a very good suit and it was made for me and it is quite similar to all my suits. Nevertheless it is a costume.

What do you think? That I am a typical product of my age and my class? Perhaps I am but so are you, and don't you, when strangers and friends come to call, straighten the cushions, kick the books under the bed and put away the letter you were writing? How many of us want any of us to see us as we really are? Isn't the mirror hostile enough?

Hide me, hide me, quiet grave. My face turned away at last. One life is quite enough to bear. Perhaps that is why I never married.

There was someone once. Someone whose fingers curled and uncurled like a fern as she slept. She slept on the river bank where the water carried her dreams away. I stood at the weir and caught them. I had no dreams of my own.

On that beat below the house I still see her, her hair down and flowing like the river, her eyes, water-blue. She glistened and shone, my hands were wet, empty and wet, with only the skin of her, her dress left behind.

Things to hide. The archive is never complete. Certain photographs are destroyed. Certain information is withheld.

My name is Samuel Wisbech. I am fifty-three. I live in the county of Dorset, England, and have done for three hundred and thirty years. We did some service to Elizabeth the First. That Queen gave us lands and buildings which were for a long time disputed. They are disputed again, this time by some gentlemen from the Tax Office.

Before we were landed we were at sea. All at sea every one of us, Flemish merchants who settled in London and ran our ships up and down the accommodating Thames.

In those days scores were settled with a knife at night. My family were murderers. Most families were. It was difficult to run a business without killing someone now and then. It still is, but we are more civilised. We don't take their lives, we take their livelihoods.

I prefer the more direct method. Don't turn away. It's just a joke. Just a joke.

You will notice that the little preamble I give my visitors is not necessarily well received. Some of them would like to leave at once and I enjoy the visible agony of mind fought out between their distaste and the fact that they have parted with £10 entrance money including tea.

The tea wins. It is waiting for them, holding out a promise of the future where all is spice buns and warmth. I am in the past with the murderers. I am a figure already receding down a corridor marked 'PRIVATE.'

PRIVATE. That's the part they really want, those visitors of mine. There's always someone ready to step silently backwards into the shadows. They duck under the ropes as though the house were a boxing ring. Who is it in the Red Corner?

Disappearance II

Me, always me, waiting for them politely. A house like this, people don't understand, a house like this is alive. They think it's closed circuit television. No, no, it's the house itself.

The other day the telephone rang and I answered it myself. I had to inform the caller that the house was not open until April. Enthusiastic by race, American, she said, 'No problem.' I took that to mean she would book herself on the first tour of the season. She took it to mean she would arrive one evening, face lively, cheque blank.

I answered the door myself. I cannot seem to find any servants at all at the moment. I answered the door. I am a gentleman. I showed her in and poured her a drink. It was not so very difficult. Perhaps I am too much alone.

My sentences were a little stilted, formal. I tried to say, 'My name is Samuel Wisbech. I am fifty-three . . .' but she held up her hand. She had heard it already, last summer on a tour, wouldn't I just talk to her, be myself?

Myself? Itself? The house, me, me the house. My voice sounds like the wind at the window. My skin is the texture of flaking plaster. I am upholstered like an old man, an old house, there is decay on us both.

What shall I say? The words here are out of date, we have never replaced them, there is no need of speech when the stones cry out. The house and I understand each other and there is no one else. I think the servants must have left long ago.

I watched my visitor taking in the room. I used her eyes. Perhaps it does look odd, the furniture cowering under dustsheets, the paintings taped over with brown paper. I did explain that we were not open.

She asked me to show her over the place, as though she were looking for a mortgage and I were an estate agent. Her voice was as bright as cut glass. She stood up on those heels of hers and we set off, the sound of her tapping like a hammer at my head, myself passing as silent as ever.

'There's plenty of work for you to do before opening day,' she said, as another door fell from its hinges.

'These rooms are private,' I said.

'But there are so many of them.'

I smiled. I was turned away from her but I smiled. The secret places pile one on top of the other like bodies in an open grave.

I showed her the revolving fireplaces, the priest's hole, the trap door, the dungeon. I showed her the kitchen and the wheel where the beagle was chained to tread endlessly and turn the spit for roasts.

'How barbaric,' she said. I nodded. Myself, I hardly eat at all these days.

'Here's the dog,' I said, opening a cupboard. A heap of dust fell out, a collar somewhere in the middle of it, worn, chewed, with a lead medallion, REX.

My visitor fainted. I thought she would.

Night came and with it the fog. The house was held in the fog's long embrace. I half carried, half dragged my visitor back towards the fire, whispering to her, stroking her hair. I told her these stories and many more. The stories I had learned from the house.

As I talked it seemed to me that the house itself was craning inwards to listen. Then I knew it was the house speaking. My lips flapped uselessly. I sat in the lap of the house. The house had its arms round me. I was safe.

April the first. Opening Day. The garden is an orchestra of flowers; strings of wild clematis, tulip flutes, a timpani of lily pads on the skin of the pond, and the raised horns of the daffodils blaring light. Spring is so noisy.

I am pleased. Pleased with the crowd at the door and the new roof for the west wing. My American visitor paid for that. We talk almost every night. She loves the place. She loves the place so much she will never leave. I have let her have mother's room. Did I mention mother's room?

. . .

My mother's room is not part of the tour. It is preserved exactly as she left it, in 1921. When she entered the stable. She was bound to keep it as my grandmother had left it, when she died in 1895. The heavy curtains, the ink well, the blotter, yes the blotter with its strange inverted message, 'I am going mad.' There is something theatrical about the female sex.

I took my visitor there on the night she arrived. I thought it unwise for her to attempt to leave in the fog. I made her as comfortable as I could, although the bed was musty and had a stain in it. I told her to ring the bell if she wanted anything. From my own quarters I heard the bell's dull clapper all night. I would speak to the servants if I could find them.

I took her breakfast the following day. I took her lunch. I thought it unwise for her to leave. We talked that night and many others, she said less and less. It is something to do with the house.

The house. How ruined it seems. How tired. Do the visitors come at all? Are they here today or was it last year, the year before? My name is Samuel Wisbech. I am fifty-three. The record is cracked. The gramophone won't play. We have no servants these days.

I went to find her. I called down the corridors of time, 'Mother, where are you, come out, the guests are here.' She didn't answer me, and the little boy ran faster, pushing open the heavy doors that swung at him like weapons.

Where was she? The house grew bigger and bigger and the room she was in faded further and further away. I saw the outline of her dress, nothing more, and the river pouring into her room.

Spring comes. The river bank flowers and the brown winter waters turn clear for the trout.

The room is there, somewhere, it must be. I can see the window from where I stand at the weir. I know the way through the house. When I go indoors to find her the house mocks me. There is no room.

They must be there somewhere, on the other side of the wall, separated from me by an inch or two at most. I can hear them laughing, the women together, laughing at me uselessly shaking the dead doors. They are all in there and I am here, caught in my house, room by room, unable to find the only room where there is peace.

The Green Man

To honour. To mock. To fear. To hate. To be fascinated. To laugh out loud.

The gypsies come here every year once a year. Come living. Come memory. Half dream. Half danger. Half man half beast. Satyr them, satire us; safe, good, time keeping, clean, for a day dragged in front of their silvered mirrors.

Get my fortune told. Buy a pony. Sharpen my knives to their murder edge. I wear my pants baggy but pass their glass and I look like a stag in rut. Down Sir! Oh cool comfort on a sunny day that my embarrassment is mine alone. The river is wide where they camp either side and I am clothed but my reflection is naked.

They breed horses. That is they breed themselves and sell off their children of the nether parts, piebald rascals all mane and tail, to set a swag at a girl. Well known it is that young girls love horses, loving the wild underside of themselves, loving the long neck and hot ears of animal seduction.

Buy the young lady a pony and the trap is thrown in free. These round-bellied glint-eyed hosses are Trojan horses. Truant, feckless, anarchic, unsaddled and munching to bare earth the ordered weekends of Daddy's life; the lawn.

Didn't Daddy save up to move out of the city? Didn't he save for a painted house and a picket fence? Didn't he save for wife and daughter? And after one long satisfactory shower of sperm hasn't his wife bottled him like a genie and taught him to spend his lust on the lawn?

Oh the suburban weekend oh!

On Friday Daddy cuts the lawn. On Saturday Daddy waters it. On Sunday Daddy barbeques on the lawn. On Monday Daddy leaves it and looks with half regret on his close-cropped green-eyed doll. His manhood is buried there and next weekend he'll spike it.

But the gypsies are coming and his daughter is thirteen.

Talk of the town is that the fair should be banned. This time could be the last time if the Mayor has his way. Time is gone when folks needed travelling play, when the bright band of gypsy caravans looping down the hill made a gold ring of holiday fire. What the gypsies sell you can buy any place and better. No one keeps their pans to copper. This town is stainless steel.

Why am I frightened by the scissor man? Why does my heart curl? The noise of the blacksmith hurts my feet and the knife grinder whets my backbone. The red-head trull selling silk will deck me in a beaded scarf. She would make me her Corn King if she could and take what little I have left. The Green Man on the green lawn sprouting ears of wheat.

My daughter came back from school and said, 'Daddy, in the Olden Days the Queen married the King and after a year she killed him.'

I said, 'I know that sweetheart.'

She said, 'It was to make the crops grow,' and I went out and worked on the lawn.

The gypsies are coming. Gutsy from the North. Open faced from the West. Beguiling from the East. South and Sexy. In less than a day's march, less than a night's scheming, by compass and constellation they will be here. Spread out the map and pinpoint me. I am voodooed head to foot.

My wife said, 'What are those punctures in your chest?'

I said, 'I fell on the spiker.'

I have taken great pains to neaten the garden. It is a triumph of restraint. Although it is summer and clematis and rose would garland my head if I let them I have clipped their easy virtue into something finer. They climb, they decorate, they do not spread. My wife admires this from her bedroom. Meanwhile, our inner and outer spheres have met at a point of mutuality. It is our daughter's birthday and the day of the fair.

When a horse pisses it locks its front legs raises its tail and drops a shaft of vast dimensions that shoots a fireman's douse. This was the first thing we saw, the three of us, as we walked hand in hand in the field.

'Daddy, look,' said my daughter and gripped my finger. The grass turned liquid. I thought, 'We shall have to swim for it.' My wife was wearing peep-toes.

A Hispanic came by selling ice creams.

'You want one?' he said, looking at the trunk of piss.

My wife paid, while my daughter and I stood helplessly together and I thought, 'She wants to touch it. Oh God.'

She broke from my hand and went up and patted the horse, dry now, shrinking up into himself. The green pool winked at us.

We walked on, a normal three-way family, eating our ice creams. I tried to win at the shooting gallery but they screw the guns. There was a woman behind me, the kind I don't like, big boots and jeans, and a slender body and a stare. She slung a gun and massacred the target. The stall keeper laughed and said something to her in their own tongue. She chose her prize and strode away with it, another girl at her arm.

'Ciao Reina,' shouted the stall keeper and I told my wife it was a put up job to fake an even chance and pull a sucker after his luck.

He gestured to me. 'Try again.'

I said, 'You screw the guns.'

He shrugged and picked up a glass rolling pin. 'Maybe your wife would like this?'

They were blowing glass at the next stall. There were men in leather aprons, their skin as thick and dark, playing on their soundless trumpets and forcing a ball of glass into the fire-shot air.

'See your future in it,' said the hag who took the money. 'Quick, now, as it comes.'

I turned away. My wife wanted to buy a witch ball for her display cabinet. I said I thought it was a mistake, 'They are just cheap stuff.' But she liked the way the colours caught in the lacunae of the surface. Reluctantly I gave the hag the money.

She caught my hand as I did so. Instinctively I closed it into a fist but she twisted it like a door knob and my fingers fell open, palm up under her greasy stare. My one hand was much bigger than both of hers together and if I were a quick bite horror writer I suppose I would call them claws. With her hooked nail she scored my heart line and laughed out loud.

'The heart stops,' she said.

'You mean I'm going to die?'

'Only your heart.'

I pulled away from her and put my hand up to my chest. My ironed cotton chest. My heart was still beating time. The two glass blowers were looking at me with open contempt, as though I were the one filthy, scarred, vagrant. I stepped backwards and collided with one of their women selling bracelets from a basket. My force spilled some of them and I bent down with her to pick them up, saying 'Sorry, sorry,' all the while. I was conscious of the others watching me. Where was my wife?

I concentrated on scooping up the last of the fakey sliding gold and raised my head. Her breasts were by my mouth. Her breasts falling out of her man's loose shirt. Her breasts, tan, taut. Her breasts, unharnessed.

She pulled my head forward and even while I was pulling away I had her skin against my upper lip and my cheeks were burning with shame and I was worrying that I hadn't shaved enough and hating myself and hating this . . .

To honour. To mock. To fear. To hate. To laugh out loud. To be fascinated.

Where was my wife?

They were laughing at me, all of them, as I scrambled off the grass and blundered away. My wife and daughter were up ahead moving at the same mesmerised pace as everyone else. I shoved through the tranced crowds and caught up with them both, their backs to me, hand in hand, my wife and daughter. I smoothed myself down and put my arms round their shoulders. My wife turned and smiled and together we watched the jugglers and my heart paced back to its normal metronome and I breathed again, not too shallow, not too deep. I began to think about a beer.

'What happened to your trousers?'

My hand went straight to my crotch but my wife did not notice. She was glaring at my knees. I let my eyes travel downwards and there were two green splotches neatly capping my white ducks.

Yes I know we have only just bought me these trousers. These trousers were expensive. These trousers are blatant in their whiteness. Sassy as a virgin courting a stain. These are bachelor trousers not gelded chinos. These are touch trousers in fourteen ounce linen and we had a fight in the shop.

Now we shall have a fight in the field and our raised voices have sawn out a circle in the crowds around us. Our daughter is embarrassed and walks away. My wife says, 'Ruined.' 'Stupid.' 'Specialist cleaning.' 'Grass.' 'How could you?' and gradually her words break up, out of their sentences, verbs and objects falling away, leaving the subject, me, me, failed again. Failure.

I could no longer hear her. Could see the words forming in glass bubbles out of the crazy trumpet of her mouth. My cartoon wife. Her cartoon husband. Waving their arms and blowing bubbles at the crowd.

.   .   .

Till death us do part. Nothing in the marriage service about a pair of stained trousers. Let me pass. A man can still have a drink can't he? I went into the beer tent where there was a pianola and a long trestle table, a merciful place to hide my knees and prop my elbows. I don't go out to bars. I'm a family man and proud of it. We like to eat together and share a bottle of wine. My wife buys it from the Family Wine Club. We usually get the Mystery Mix and it's always the same. I would prefer beer but I don't do the shopping.

Sometimes, when I leave for work early in the morning and my wife and daughter are still asleep, I truly believe that I will never come back. I love them both, sincerely I do, and I can't explain how you can love a thing and want to be parted from it forever. Sometimes I wish she would kill me, collect the insurance, go on with her life and free me from the guilt of staying, the guilt of going.

A friend of mine did go and now he lives in a rented place in the city, two rooms and no responsibilities and he is about as miserable as before. Change your life, they tell me, in those popular New Age Bibles, and my wife and I both understand the importance of speaking the truth and we have learned about quality time. Yet when I look at her and when she looks at me our eyes are pale.

What's in your eyes darling? What do I see? The daily calculations of money and sex. How much of one, how little of the other, the see-saw of married life, keep the balance just. Keep the balance, just. I am a heterosexual male. My wife is a heterosexual female. Are we too normal to enjoy our bed?

Normal male to Norman Mailer: Please tell me how.

Have you ever had a boy? I'd like to but I can't do it.

Listen to me. A man will try anything or thinks he will. I talk like a tomcat but I act like a worm. What happened to youth and glory? What happened to those bright days when the sun was still rising? Soon it will be Midsummer and the light beginning to die back, imperceptibly at first, a few minutes a day, and then the gradual forcing back indoors earlier and earlier, helpless against the dark.

Midsummer used to be a fire festival. They used to light the bonfires on Midsummer night and burn them through June 24, Midsummer Day. Maybe they thought they could prop up the sun in his luminary ride. Hold him in the heavens at his peak. It was a night of visions and strange dreams. A night of lawlessness, for the Corn King, the Green Man, could copulate with whomsoever he pleased. For a spell time stopped. At the moment of decline accelerate. Call it a wild perversity or a wild optimism, but they were right, our ancestors, to celebrate what they feared. What I fear I avoid. What I fear I pretend does not exist. What I fear is quietly killing me. Would there were a festival for my fears, a ritual burning of what is coward in me, what is lost in me. Let the light in before it is too late.

The gypsies have come down the hill, their eyes in burning hoops. Come pony tail, come pony. Come highwater, come Hell. The river has risen with summer rain, rain in steam clouds above their fires. Fires infernal, fires illegal, bursts of water, bursts of flame.

The Mayor says it will have to be stopped. This is a Conservation Area. No dumping. No overnight camping. No fishing. No fires. No hawking. No begging. No talking after lights-out. No sickness without medical insurance. No travel without passports. No status without a bank account. No welfare without a job. No flirting. No slacking. No drugs. No Queers (maybe rich ones). No foreigners (maybe rich ones or cheap ones).

The gypsies are here. Eyes the colour of stars. Dressed in history. Dressed in rainbows. Some wear jerkins, some wear knee breeches, some wear swami robes, some wear cowhide coats. All wear gold and not the kind they sell. The men look like pirates. The women look like whores. Tall women, heads back, bold stare, easy hips. What right have they to walk as if they have never known pain? Do you watch the way people walk? I do. I look for the disappointments in their shoulders and the stress in their hips. Look for the slight limp that betrays their vulnerable side. What kind of man or woman they are is in their gait. I never give a man a job until I've seen the way he walks. I courted my wife because when she moved she seemed to take the earth with her.

What happened to us holding hands side by side? Somewhere in the fourteen years of our married life I seem to have had a sex change and converted to Islam. How else to explain the twenty paces I lag behind?

When I come home caught in the cobwebs of my day, my wife has been planning our next holiday or working out the finance for a new car. I am still building the extension she designed two years ago. I have to fit it in with my job and the garden and time for my daughter who loves me. My wife strides us on into prosperity and fulfilment and I shuffle behind clutching the bills and a tool box. She was right to make me drain the lawn. All our friends admire its rollered curves. I admire my wife. Admire our success. We were nothing and she has coaxed out the grit in me and held me to my job. Why do I wish we were young again and she would hold me in her arms?

Listen to me. I sound like the fool I am. Fortunately I am alone.

At that moment I looked up out of the comforting opacity of my beer and down the trestle table. Tightly packed, like rowers in a slave ship, were a couple of hundred men, heads on their fists, staring into their beer as if it were a crystal ball. And the table seemed to infinitely extend through the candy striped canvas and out over the hills into the city and to be forever lined with men.

I got to my feet and left through an open flap at the back of the tent. I was away from the bustle of the fair and out by a few caravans, their fires pushing up smoke. Sitting beside one of the fires was the woman I had met already.

She said, 'Take off your trousers.'

'What?'

'I'll clean them for you.'

She turned her back and went up the wooden steps into a caravan. I was about twenty paces behind.

When I finally hesitated myself inside she was pouring blue powder into a copper pot. The caravan was one of those old barrel types with a pair of long shafts for the horse to draw it. Inside it was panelled, carved, sprung, beautiful, clean. She had a feather eiderdown on the bed and the bed was how a bed should be. Not too hygienic, not too hospital, not a showroom bed with matching sheets and pillow cases.

She held out her hand for my trousers and I wondered how her hair seemed so red that when she leaned over the copper there was no distinction between the soft metal and her soft hair.

She smiled and looked down at me. Not at my knees. I had my shirt tails but it was obvious how things stood. I suppose it was obvious how things were going to be but when I bucked into her it was with the same surprise as all those years ago when Alison and I had walked in the woods and made love among the bluebells. I had the perfect freedom of loving her and although we have never given up sex we never have found those woods again.

I felt the trees closing over me and I slept.

It was dark when I woke up. I was alone in the bed. I sat up and grabbed the cover around me. Gradually I could make out the shapes in the caravan and I found an oil lamp with its wick just burning under the brass cover. I turned it up and on the chair beside it were my trousers neatly folded and dry.

I inspected the knees. The accusing stains had disappeared but was it a trick of the light or were the trousers all over now hued invisible green? I dressed as quickly as I could and let myself out of the caravan.

What time was it? I checked my wrist and found my watch had gone. Should I go back in? I couldn't. I wanted to be away, be home, not be noticed, not be caught. I still had my wallet.

As I set off through the fields towards the empty stalls I saw by the firelight a group of men leading a horse up and down. There was a girl on it, clinging to the mane, slithering a bit on the bare back. I changed direction to avoid them but then I heard the girl shout, 'Daddy! Daddy!' I started running towards her voice and forgetting everything that had happened I burst through the blanks of the men to the only thing that mattered and swept my daughter off the horse and into my arms. The men were laughing.

'What are you doing here?' I said. 'Where's Mummy?'

'The young lady has bought a horse,' said one of the men.

My daughter kissed me and said something about her birthday and in my swimming head drowned in horse piss and laundry blue, another woman's body and my own tears, I thought, 'I have to get us out of here, I must get us home.' I took her hand and we walked slowly away, me as cautious as a cat but unfollowed. One of the men shouted, 'We will bring him tomorrow.'

And I didn't care because they didn't know me or where we lived and the fair would move on and my daughter would forget and I would forget.

My wife was watching late night TV.

She said, 'Do you know what time it is?'

My daughter and I, hand in hand, looked at each other and each sheltered secrets the other half shared but could not betray.

The nights are short at this time of year; a reluctant darkness and a terrace of stars near enough to walk upon, as the gods used to do, before the light rinses the sky.

At dawn, around four o'clock, I was dozing, still dressed on the green lawn, my wife and daughter sound asleep upstairs, when I heard a clip clopping coming down the road in front of the house. Shiny noise of shod horse. I thought the hooves were going through my heart. I jumped up and took a short cut through the tool shed round to the front garden.

'Don't wake up please don't wake up,' I prayed to the motionless windows.

The sky was turning laundry blue and the copper sun through it. She was standing quite still, smiling at me, holding the horse by its halter. A bright Bay the colour of her. I thought, 'I could leave now and not come back. Grow a pony tail and wear a cowhide coat,' and my mind bucked into hers with the force of the morning unworn by any but ourselves. There was a noise behind me and my daughter came up beside me in her old dressing gown. She put her hand in mine just as the horse braced its forelegs and serenely shot its piss onto the clipped verge.

The gypsy woman named her sum, an amount as extravagant as unaffordable, and I shooed my daughter back inside with me while I fetched the cash. I had drawn it out on Friday as down payment on my wife's new car. The woman had tethered the horse to the fence post, and I on one side, she on the other, exchanged the money. I noticed she was wearing my watch. Then, as she counted the last notes and I withdrew my hand, she took it swiftly, put it on her breast where her heart beat and kissed me.

My own heart stopped as she turned and walked away up the empty road.

Turn of the World

At the turn of the world are four islands.

Their names are Fyr, Hydor, Aeros, Erde.

Each of these islands is distinct in character and if none has been fully mapped all have been described. What follows is a leaf among the whirl of leaves torn from trees and books by the four winds that blow over the islands and bring their reputations to the haunts of men.

The island of Fyr.

A volcanic island thrown out of the earth's crust. What was deep is high. What was hidden is visible for all to see. The red peaks of Fyr are a landmark and a warning. No one knows when the island will erupt again, spilling itself in furious melt into the burning sea.

Naturally enough this island is stocked with lions the colour of gold and gold the colour of lions. The yellow sun shines on both and butters the hearts of the unwary who come here. Many are devoured. Many are spent. The lions are ruthless as money. The gold is snap-jawed.

Arum lilies grow here, trumpets blaring light, gunpowder stamens and a flint stalk. The lilies of the field neither toil nor spin but from time to time they explode, strewing the ground with a shrapnel of petals; force, fuse, flower.

To eat, there are carrots, pumpkins, sweet pepper, chillies, tomatoes, red onions, ruby chard, oranges, raspberries, red currants, and a Snow White apple, which of course is red.

To drink, there is wine from the grapes on the vine; Pinot Noir, crushed blood-black. The streams flow fire-water.

Anyone who cooks simply throws their food onto a hot stone. Anyone who sleeps must sleep suspended in a hammock above the heat-charged rocks.

At the heart of the island is a mystery. Everyone knows about it, though most have forgotten and few have ever seen it. Travellers to the island stuff their pockets with coins from the beach, only to find too late that the yellow stuff is sand. Others, who don't care for the money, safari the lions. There are trails of men, crawling elbows and stomach through the thick and thickening undergrowth of time. Constantly, they synchronise their watches, judging the moment of kill, while the sun on the sun-dial impassively gathers the years they have left behind.

The sound of shot, the clinking of coins, are the island's quick noises. Only as the traveller moves inwards, which he and she must do concentrically, because of the rocks, do the noises seem more distant, seem to fade.

At the heart of the island, at the point of zero coordinates, is a ring of serpentine fire. The fire has never been lit and will never be extinguished. It burns.

At the centre of the unlit blazing fire are a man and a

woman, back to back, holding hands. They do not move. Do they breathe? They stare ahead, she to the East, he to the West, intent through millennia, at the pause of time.

The traveller who can, and who can? moves face to face around the twinned royal pair and the ancientness of what he sees frightens him. The pair are youthful but older than the fire in which they wait and the fire has burned forever.

Whose face does the traveller see? His own.

Whose face does the traveller see? Her own.

Male and female, like for like, separate and identical. A man's face in the woman's. A woman's face in the man's, and both faces the face of the traveller.

The island of Hydor.

This island is submerged by water. In some parts, the shelves of land cannot be determined at all. In other places, a person may wade or paddle easily and see all that there is to see just beneath the surface.

To explore the island well, it is necessary to swim and to dive and to travel by rowing boat. Outboard motors too easily break the clarity of the water, and while further distances can be travelled, nothing of any worth can be discovered, because what the island offers is beneath.

The island is chiefly visited for its cooling, healing, shallower shore waters, and its fresh springs which refresh and cleanse. Even the inhabitants of Fyr visit occasionally to soothe their red faces and to bathe their wounds. The inhabitants of Hydor make a living bottling their spas and selling fish and they are known too, for expertise in clairvoyance.

There are three regions: The Shore. The Lakes. The Deep. At the shore, with its bustle of nets and crabs, bottles and booths, men and women roll up their trousers, and shrimp in the friendly waters. Here are rock pools and pleasant bays, teasing, hospitable. Lie down, and the water is snug as a blanket. The days are long. Fyr is visible across the channel and the shoreline of Hydor enjoys Fyr's sun.

The region of the lakes is stranger.

Willows and alders grow at the margins of huge stretches of still and connected water. Brown trout dawdle beneath the water's skin.

There is little sun here. The moon, crescent, full, waned, is always visible and reflected in the water. The waters themselves might be moons, so luminous they seem.

The traveller by boat has few landmarks. The lift and fall of the oars are the only sound, the only movement, to comfort the solitary rower. It is as though all the waters of the earth are here, illimitable, dark. That which rose from the waters at last returned to it, without form, void.

There are shapes in the water. Fantastic turrets and crenellations. The remnants of a flag. At night, the rower imagines that he sees fires burning at the bottom of the lakes. He longs to plunge down, into forgetfulness, away from memory, his life washed off him, clean at last. The lakes are full of abandoned boats.

It becomes harder to row. The fluid waters seem fast as steel. The agony of rise and fall, the strength to pull forward, the clang of the oars on the metal surface of the lake, all become hypnotic. The boat noses through the water's stars.

There is a horrible drop. The boat will be tossed over a cataract and smashed to bits. If the rower, falling in vertical terror, can survive the ceaseless roar, she finds herself floating towards a small natural well.

This well, the island's deep centre, beyond the shore, beyond the lakes, is a mandala of pure water. By its side is an urn. In the well itself are two fishes, one red, one blue.

She lies down and looks into the well. She sees her face, her many faces, masks drawn through time. She sees her face since time began. She sees all the world in the enveloping waters and remembers everything. She sees the beginning and the end swimming after each other.

There is no beginning. There is no end. The water is unbroken.

The island of Erde.

Here are mines and jewels. The climate of Erde is blustery and damp with frequent snow fall in the long winter. To keep warm, the inhabitants have perfected a cast-iron stove that burns diamonds. Diamonds are the cheapest fuel source on Erde. The coal seams are so ancient and undug that their carbon is no longer carbonaceous rock but crystallised carbon. Anyone who foots a spade into the earth will find a shovelful of uncut diamonds, which will burn unattended for two weeks.

It is true that certain mines on the island are still young, and these are highly prized. The richest women wear coal earrings and coal necklaces and the coal merchants of Erde are the wealthiest men in the world. Tourists are taken round the filthy, black coal-cutting studios near the mines, and marvel at the treasures on display. The King of Erde has a crown made entirely of coal, including the largest lump of coal ever brought up from the coveted mine. The cut lump is two feet by three feet and weighs as much as a Tamworth Sow. On state occasions, when the precious crown is carefully blacked and sooted, four men must walk beside the king to support the fabulous glory. To be covered in coal-dust is thought a great honour.

For the most part though, the people are modest and content, sitting quietly by their winter fires, poking the diamonds.

Visitors to the island come for the caving and the hunting. The underground passages of Erde are hung with stalactites and furnished with stalagmites. Carving is a national hobby, and the growths of minerals, deep in the caves, have been fashioned into beds and chairs, elephants and whales, making a world within a world. Cavers drink their coffee out of fossil cups.

Beasts of every kind still roam Erde and hunting parties are organised throughout the season. The guides and beaters are strict; no one must stray from the route. If the prey reaches the interior, it is given up for lost.

There have been stories of foolhardy hunters who have rushed ahead into unmarked places of Erde, and they have never returned. The guides are silent. No search party is sent out. The guides themselves would not return.

What is the mystery of Erde? It is said that when a man or a woman of that place has done all they wish to do in the world, they set off, without warning, drawn as if by a magnet, towards the interior.

If the people of Hydor are known for clairvoyance, the people of Erde are known for prophesy. It is said that the Norns live in the interior, weaving their fateful rope.

Perhaps they do. The traveller has seen three sisters beckoning to him, as he nears the magnetic pole of the island. There is a tree there, whose top stretches up to heaven and whose roots push down to hell. The tree is eloquent. In its branches seem to be the tracings of the whole world. The traveller rubs his hands against the thick bark and his hands are sapped with time. He puts his head against the tree, glad to rest, and hears the rumble of history coursing through the trunk.

Perhaps it is the World Ash Tree. Perhaps it is the tree of

the knowledge of good and evil. Perhaps it is the alchemists' tree, under whose shade the self will grow again. The traveller does not know but he starts to climb.

The island of Aeros.

Where to begin? Aeros is not to be found in the same place for a week together. There are stories of travellers who set out to find the island, and when they arrive at where their destination should be, the island has gone.

The people of Aeros use their island like a magic carpet, propelling it first here, then there, packing up at a moment's notice, disappearing with quicksilver grace. To their credit, they usually leave a note pinned in mid-air.

To find the island it is necessary to travel by plane, balloon, or to carry an extension ladder. The island hovers. Many a person has discovered it, only to find that it remains out of reach.

The four winds home here. The mountain air of the region develops the lungs of the inhabitants, who are known for singing, juggling, making musical instruments, and building elaborate windmills to tilt at. This is a talkative island, and when they are not talking to each other, the inhabitants shout encouragement at the other islands, as Aeros flies by.

The constant movement of the place is such that solider travellers complain a rough sea is stiller.

The people of Aeros are great story-tellers. Even the simplest action is bound into a story. It is common for a queue of people, waiting for a cable car, to become so much part of the story they are hearing, that they transform themselves into it. Only last week, a dozen listeners, intent on the story of 'How the Genie was trapped in the Copper Vase,' forgot their own lives entirely. Six of them became the genie, and sat wrapped up, as if in a vase, while half a dozen became the market stall holder who bought the copper vase by mistake.

The city rerouted the cable car stop, and the story-teller was left to run through the streets, bringing the families of the transformed to join their new lives.

No one worries. Sooner or later, another story, more powerful than the last, will free them; free them into other selves or back into their own.

And this is part of the mystery.

As one travels through the island, street by street, mountain by mountain, story by story, it is the stories that begin to dominate. A man sits down, cooks himself a story and eats it. A woman falls asleep on a bed of stories, a story drawn up to her chin.

Deeper into the island, where the cable cars stop and where the nimble ponies are left far behind, the only way for anyone to travel is by story.

Some stories go farther than others. Some take the traveller as far as the line of mountains bordering a vast forest.

At this place, lonely and silent, the story falters. The traveller turns to look back at the distance and while he or she is busy with other thoughts, the stories disappear into the forest from where they came.

It is well known that all the stories in the world come from this dense dark forest, come out of the regions of silence into the government of the tongue. Anyone who sits for long enough and narrows his eyes on the strip of forest he can penetrate will see strange shapes movi ng in the half-light. Is that Hercules in a lion skin? Is that Icarus waxed into golden wings? Is that Siegfried's horn in the distance? Is that Lancelot's horse?

The traveller is tired now, and thinks he sees dwarves carrying iron hammers, and the old witch Baba Yaga stirring at her brew. He seems to hear the fi, fie, fo of the giants, and to smell trolls coming home though the wood.

The wind is up, carrying the Snow Queen across the frozen stars, the red sun sinks beyond the trees.

The traveller reaches out a hand to catch the sun and catches a chestnut. The case has split and the nut is smooth and burnished, giving out a faint light. He puts it in his pocket. She puts it in her pocket. They walk down into the closure of the forest, until they too become part of the story.

Newton

This is the story of Tom.

This is the story of Tom and his neighbours.

This is the story of Tom and his neighbours and his neighbour's garden.

This is the story of Tom.

'All of my neighbours are Classical Physicists,' said Tom. 'Their laws of motion are determined. They rise at 7 a.m. and leave for work at 8 a.m. The women take coffee at 10 a.m. If you see a body on the street between 1 and 2 p.m. lunchtime, it can only be the doctor, it can only be the undertaker, it can only be the stranger.

'I am the stranger,' said Tom.

'What is the First Law of Thermodynamics?' said Tom.

'You can't transfer heat from a colder to a hotter. I've never known any warmth from my neighbours so I would reckon this is true. Here in Newton we don't talk much. That is, my neighbours talk all the time, they swap gossip, but I never have any, although sometimes I am some.'

.   .   .

'What is the Second Law of Thermodynamics?' said Tom.

'Everything tends towards the condition of entropy. That is, the energy is still there somewhere but for all useful purposes it is lost. Take a look at my neighbours here in Newton and you'll see what it means.'

My neighbour has a garden full of plastic flowers. 'It's easy,' she says, 'and so nice.' When her husband died she had him laminated, and he stands outside now, hands on his hips, carefully watching the sky.

'What's the matter Tom?' she says, her head bobbing along the fence like a duck in a shooting parlour.

'Why don't you get married? In my day nobody had any trouble finding someone. We just did it and made the best of it. There were no screwballs then.'

'What none?'

She bobbed faster and faster, gathering a bosom-load of underwear from the washing line. I knew she wanted me to stare at it, she wants to prove that I am a screwball. After all, if it's me, it's not her, it's not the others. You can't have more than one per block.

She wheeled round, ready to bob back up the other way, knickers popping from every pore.

'Tom, we were glad to be normal. In those days it was something good, something to be proud of.'

.   .   .

Tom the screwball. Here I am with my paperback foreign editions and my corduroy trousers ('You got something against Levi's?' he asked me, before he was laminated). All the men round here wear Levi's, denims or chinos. The only stylistic difference is whether they pack their stomach inside or outside the waistband.

They suspect me of being a homosexual. I wouldn't care. I wouldn't care what I was if only I were something.

'What do you want to be when you grow up?' said my mother, a long time ago, many times a long time ago.

'A fireman, an astronaut, a spy, a train driver, a hard hat, an inventor, a deep sea diver, a doctor and a nurse.'

'What do you want to be when you grow up?' I ask myself in the mirror most days.

'Myself. I want to be myself.'

And who is that, Tom?

Into the clockwork universe the quantum child. Why doesn't every mother believe her child can change the world? The child can. This is the joke. Here we are still looking for a saviour and hundreds are being born every second. Look at it, this tiny capsule of new life, indifferent to your prejudices, your miseries, unmindful of the world already made. Make it again? They could if we let them, but we make sure they grow up just like us, fearful like us. Don't let them know the potential that they are. Don't let them hear the grass singing. Let them live and die in Newton, tick-tock, the last breath.

There was a knock at my door, I hid my Camus in the fridge and peered through the frosted glass. Of course I can't see anything. They never remind you of that when you fit frosted glass.

'Tom? Tom?' RAP RAP.

It's my neighbour. I shuffled to the door, feet bare, shirt loose. There she is, her hair coiled on her head like a wreath on a war memorial. She was dressed solely in pink.

'I'm not interrupting am I Tom?' she said, her eyes shoving past me into the kitchen.

'I was reading.'

'That's what I thought. I said to myself, poor Tom will be reading. He won't be busy. I'll ask him to help me out. You know how difficult it is for a woman to manage alone. Since my husband was laminated, I haven't had it easy, Tom.'

She smelled of woman; warm, perfumed, slightly threatening. I had to be careful not to act like a screwball. I offered her coffee. She seemed pleased, although she kept glancing at my bare feet and loose shirt. Never mind, she needs me to help her with something in the house. That's normal, that's nice, I want to be normal and nice.

'My mother's here. Will you help me get her into the house.'

'Now? Shall we go now?'

'She's had a long journey. She can rest in the truck a while. Shall we have that coffee you offered me first?'

I don't love my neighbour but still my hand trembled over the sugar spoon. They've made me feel odd and outside for so long, that now even the simplest things feel strange.

How does a normal person make coffee? What is it about me that worries them so much? I'm clean. I have a job.

'Tom, tell me, is it the modern thing to keep books in the refrigerator?'

In cheap crime novels, you often read the line, 'He spun round.' It makes me laugh to imagine a human being so animated, but when she asked me that question, I spun. One second I was facing the sink, the next second I was facing her, and she was facing me, holding my copy of Camus.

'I was just fetching out the milk Tom. Who is Albert K Mew?' She pronounced it like an enraged cat.

'He's a Frenchman. A French writer. I don't know how he came to be in the fridge.'

She repeated my words slowly as though I had just offered her a universal truth.

'You don't know how he came to be in the fridge?' I shrugged and smiled and tried to disarm her.

'It's a big fridge. Don't you ever find things in the fridge you had forgotten about?'

'No Tom. Never. I store cheese at the top, and then beer and bacon underneath, and underneath those I keep my weekend chicken, and at the bottom I have salad things and eggs. Those are the rules. It was the same when my husband was alive and it is the same now.'

I was beginning to regard her with a new respect. The Grim Reaper came to call. He took her husband from the bed but left the weekend chicken on the shelf.

O Death, where is thy sting?

My neighbour, still holding my Camus, leaned forward confidentially, her arms resting on the table. She looked intimate, soft, I could see the beginning of her breasts.

'Tom, have you ever wondered whether you need help?' She said HELP with four capital letters, like a doorstep evangelist.

'If you mean the fridge, anyone can make a mistake.' She leaned forward a little further. More breast.

'Tom, I'm going to be tough with you. You know what your problem is? You read too many geniuses. I don't know if Mr K Mew is a genius but the other day you were seen in the main square reading Picasso's notebooks. Children were coming out of school and you were reading Picasso. Miss Fin at the library tells me that all you ever borrow are works of genius. She has no record of you ever ordering a sea story. Now that's unhealthy. Why is it unhealthy? You yourself are not a genius, if you were we would have found out by now. You are ordinary like the rest of us and ordinary people should lead ordinary lives. Like the rest of us, here in Tranquil Gardens.'

She leaned back, her bosom with her.

'Shall we go and help your mother?' I said.

Outside, my neighbour walked towards a closed van parked in front of her house. I'd seen her mother a couple of years previously but I couldn't see her now.

'She's in the back Tom. Go round the back.'

My neighbour flung open the back doors of the hired van and certainly there was her mother, sitting upright in the wheel-chair that had been her home and her car. She was smiling a fearful plasticy smile, her teeth as perfect as a cheetah's.

'Haven't they done a wonderful job Tom? She's even better than Doug, and he was pretty advanced at the time. I wish she could see herself. She never guessed I'd laminate her. She'd be so proud.'

'Are those her own teeth?'

'They are now Tom.'

'Where will you put her?'

'In the garden with the flowers. She loved flowers.'

. . .

Slowly, slowly, we heaved down mother. We wheeled her over the swept pavement to the whitewashed house. It was afternoon coffee time and a lot of neighbours had been invited to pay their respects. They were so respectful that we were outside talking plastic until the men came home. My neighbour gets an incentive voucher for every successful lamination she introduces. She reckons that if Newton will only do it her way, she'll have 75 percent of her own lamination costs paid by the time she dies.

'I've seen you hanging around the cemetery Tom. It's not hygienic.'

What does she think I am? A ghoul? I've told her before that my mother is buried there but she just shakes her head and tells me that young couples need the land.

'Until we learn to stop dying Tom, we have to live with the consequences. There's no room for the dead unless you treat them as ornamental.'

I have tried to tell her that if we stop dying, all the cemeteries in the world can never release enough land for the bulging, ageing population. She doesn't listen, she just looks dreamy and thinks about the married couples.

Newton is jammed with married couples. We need one-way streets to let the singles through. I hate going shopping in Newton. I hate clubbing my way through the crocodile files, two by two in Main street, as though the ark has landed. Complacent shoulder blades, battered baby buggys. DIY stores crammed with HIM and shopping malls heaving with HER. Don't they know that too much role playing is bad for the health? Imagine being a wife and saying 'Honey, have you got time to fix the toilet?' Imagine being a husband and figuring out how to clean the toilet when she's left you.

Why are they married? It's normal, it's nice. They do it the way they do everything else in Newton. Tick-tock says the clock.

'Tom, thank you Tom,' she cooed at me when her mother was safely settled beside the duck pond. The ducks are bathtime yellow with chirpy red beaks and their pond has real water with a bit of chlorine in it just in case. I had never been in my neighbour's garden before. It was quiet. No rustling in the undergrowth. No undergrowth to rustle in. No birds yammering. She tells me that peace is what the countryside is all about.

'If you were a genius Tom you could work here. The silence. The air. I have a unit you know, filters the air as it enters the garden.'

It was autumn and there were a few plastic leaves scattered about on the AstroTurf. At the bottom of the garden, my neighbour has a shed, made of imitation wood, where she keeps her stocks for the changing of the seasons. She has told me many times that a garden must have variety and in her ventilated Aladdin's cave are the reassuring copies of nature. Tulips, red and white, hang meekly upside down by their stems. Daffodils in bright bunches are jumbled with loose camellia blooms, waiting to be slotted into the ever-lasting tree. She even has a row of squirrels clutching identical nuts.

'Those are going out soon, along with the autumn creeper.' She has Virginia Creeper cascading down the house. It's still green. This is the burnt and blazing version.

'Mine's turning already,' I said.

'Too early,' she said. 'You can't depend on nature. I don't like leaves falling. They don't fall where they should. If you don't regulate nature, why, she'll just go ahead and do what she likes. We have to regulate her. If we don't, it's volcanoes and forest fires and floods and death and bodies scattered everywhere, just like leaves.'

Like leaves. Just like leaves. Don't you like them just a little where they fall? Don't you turn them over to see what is written on the other side? I like that. I like the simple text that can be read or not, that lies beneath your feet and mine, read or not. That falls, rain and wind, though nobody scoops it up to take it home. Life fell at your feet and you kicked her away and she bled on your shoes and when you came home, your mother said, 'Look at you, covered in leaves.'

You were covered in leaves. You peeled them off one by one, exposing the raw skin beneath. All those leavings. And when what had to fall was fallen, you picked it up and read what was written on the other side. It made no sense to you. You screwed it up in your pocket where it burned like a live coal. Tell me why they left you, one by one, the ones you loved? Didn't they like you? Didn't they, like you, need a heart that was a book with no last page? Turn the leaves.

'The leaves are turning,' said Tom.

She asked me back to supper as a thank you, and I thought I should go because that's what normal people do; eat with their neighbours, even though it is boring and the food is horrible. I searched for a tie and wore it.

'Tom, come in, what a lovely surprise!'

She must mean what a lovely surprise for me. It can hardly be a surprise for her, she's been cooking all afternoon.

Once inside the dining room, I know she means me. I know that because the entire population of Newton is already seated at the dinner table, a table that begins crammed up against the display cabinet of Capodimonte and extends . . . and extends . . . through a jagged hole blown in the side of the house, out and on towards the bus station.

'I think you know everyone Tom,' says my neighbour. 'Sit here, by me, in Doug's place. You're about his height.' Do I know everyone? It's hard to say, since beyond the hole, all is lost.

'Tom, take a plate. We're having chicken cooked in bacon strips and stuffed with hard-boiled eggs. There's a salad I made and plenty of cheese and beer in the fridge if you want it.'

She drifted away from me, her dress clinging to her like a drowned man. Nobody looked up from their plates. They were eating chicken, denims and chinos all, eating the three or four hundred fowl laid on the table, half a dozen eggs per ass. I was still trying to work out the roasting details, the oven size, when BAM, one of the chickens exploded, pelting my neighbour with eggs like hand-grenades. One of her arms flew off but luckily for her, not the one she needed for her fork. Nobody noticed. I wanted to speak, I wanted to act, I began to speak, to act, just as my neighbour herself returned carrying a covered silver dish.

'It's for you Tom,' she says, as the table falls silent. Already on my feet I was able to lift the huge lid with some dignity. Underneath was a chicken.

'It's your chicken Tom.'

She's telling the truth. Poking out of the ass of the chicken, I can see my copy of *L'Etranger* by Albert Camus. It hasn't been shredded, so I can take it out. When I open it I see that there are no words left on any of the pages. The pages are blank.

'We wanted to help you Tom.' Her eyes are full of tears. 'Not just me. All of us. A helping hand for Tom.'

Slowly the table starts to clap, faster and louder. The table shakes, the dishes roll from side to side like the drunken tableware in a sea story. This is a sea story. The captain and the crew have gone mad and I am the only passenger. Reeling, I ran from the dining room into the kitchen and slammed the door behind me. Here was peace. Hygienic enamelled peace.

Tom slid to the floor and cried.

Time passed. In Newton it always does and everyone knows how long it takes for time to pass and so nobody gets confused. Tom didn't know how much time had passed. He woke from an aching sleep and put his fist through the frosted glass kitchen door. He went home and took his big coat and filled the pockets with books and the books seemed like live coals to him. He walked away from Newton, but he did look back once, and what he saw was a table stretching out past the bend in the road and on through the streets and houses joining them together in an orgy of matching cutlery. World without end.

'But now,' says Tom, 'the hills are ripe and the water leaps at my throat when I shave.'

Tick-tock says the clock in Newton.

Holy Matrimony

My fiancé and I would like to be married in church; an ordinary hypocritical sentimental impulse from two people who do not believe in God.

My fiancé and I would like to be married in church but this is proving difficult because the people who do believe in God are selling them.

Now I know that Jean-Paul Sartre and Mr Camus were right when they claimed it is the Absurd that obtains. The Absurd, with a most capital A, that declares in this Year of our no longer Lord that unbelievers still wish to use the churches the faithful have denied. What you sell reveals what you value. The Church must be accountable. Why should I care? Why should you? But what then for my spirit now that every spirit-thing has been price-tagged?

Pity St Peter. Pity the charred ranks of martyrs, their fired bodies in the cool earth. Pity uncounted sacrifices and recorded zeal, work of hands and hearts to raise monuments in stone to the Invisible. Pity those who could not guess that to convert the unconverted the latter day Church would hire an architect.

Lengthen my stride. How long a stretch to get away from the insistence of the past? The past, ripped out, pulled down, sold off. What my parents were and what my grandparents were, and further back, through time, landmarks of a people built on more than rock, built out of bone, the framework of a commonwealth, a commonweal. What you inherited and what you were to leave behind. A thousand years of history and an island faith.

My fiancé and I will get married in a consecrated tent. This tent will be supplied and erected for the day by Dazzle Bros. Matrimonial Ltd. and all proceedings under canvas will be blessed by the Flying Vicar. These Persons of the Cloth, strategically based and conveniently close to rail and air terminals, will travel at speed and First Class to any wedding funeral or christening to offer that special touch of godliness. Video and details 0800 666.

Lengthen my stride. Walk as fast as I can, north, south, east, west. Do some complain of tinnitus? The bells are ringing across the city, faster, faster, my back to the bells, the bells at my back, each vertebra live-notched to the scale where the past still hammers its communal note. The round metallic sound of warning, of death, of summoning, of celebration. The hollow bell, and in it, teeming life. Look up; the towers are swarming.

It is not so. The light on the copper is killed. The bells

have been carted away to back lots on film sets, museums municipal and maritime, well groomed gardens in need of a folly, even as sculpture in a concrete park. Forgetting, all, that a bell's business is to ring.

The Reverend Wreck. Trap jawed, a guffaw man who likes a belly laugh and owns the necessary surface area. Monkish habit, salesman's eyes and a worrying twitch of the right hand that he claims he picked up whilst in India, unlike the left which he bought at a car boot sale. I believe that Dazzle Matrimonial supply the jokes.

The Reverend Wreck says that he will marry me. Not personally of course, another baboon snort here, but gladly, legally and cheaply. He is Budget and we both know that I cannot afford Somerset's Canon Snap. No vulgar money talk here, the vulgar Dazzle's will see to all that, and for my kind attention in due course.

The Reverend Wreck will counsel me by video on marriage and its duties, marriage and its pleasures, marriage and its pleasures and the consequences thereof. Nine months to be exact are his last words before he flickers out in a blizzard of clerical adverts. If I want him back I will have to find another penny for his slot. Do you remember those fairground peep-show machines? *Folies Bergère* and *What the Butler Saw*. I never had enough money to get past her knickers. Now I have a credit card and the Reverend Wreck.

. . .

Lengthen my stride. Buy a wedding bell for good luck. Little, lacquered, lost its clapper, wall mounting hostess model, hostess mounting wall model. Pocket pigmy dumb to say that much more than a bell has been melted away.

Progress Progress. I am getting married. Spiritually speaking we shall unite as one flesh but for all practical purposes my husband will remain a cut above me.

'Do you take this woman to be your lawful wedded Sunday joint? Will you roll her and bone her garnish and consume her? She has been sealed in her juices unto this perfect day. Please, sit down and eat, we are all cannibals now.'

Marriage. The waste paper basket of the emotions? My love poems, my diary jottings, my billet-doux, jetted into you, or if not you, what you represent: Approval, security, companionship, children, a piggy bank, a sex toy, an action man in a stagnant world.

Till death do us part. Will you update me darling? Will I go the way of all your other worldly goods? There is so much pressure on you to move with the times and I admit that I will lag behind, not least in my bosom, gravity's friend. The hands on the clock hour by hour drag me down, 'Your wife is ticking Sir, crossing off the minutes with unfeminine haste. Sir, regard her fingers moving round her face, surely her hour is at hand?'

. . .

Progress progress. More and more people want an old fashioned wedding. The new slim-line Church is doing a roaring
trade, not least because the lion had lain down with the
lamb to create that genetically engineered beast that used to
be called a Wolf in Sheep's clothing.

Now, now, don't be bitter, the Church must march ahead,
no matter that the flock has been lost. In any case, flocks
cost money, much better to kill the fatted calf and charge
for it.

A rose by any other name is not England. There is something to be said for words. Change the words and you will
change the meaning, perhaps not today or tomorrow, but
the day after, and what we thought we could keep without
valuing it will be gone. A thousand years of history and an
island faith.

Is that the bell? I would like to say 'I will.' I would like the
sincerity of a promise others have kept. I would like to
know that brick by brick, stone by stone, heart by heart, my
country, my city, my town, my village, my house, myself, will
not be taken away. My ancestors lived in a place their ancestors could recognise. I can recognise less and less. It moves
so fast, my modern world, blurring what detail is left. No
wonder I seek for certainty in your face.

It is not enough. You were not designed to be my landscape or my life-line, nor I yours. Adam and Eve to each other, perhaps, but with fruit trees and animals between and with someone else who walked in the Garden, and who called us by name.

What can a human being do? The men in dog collars no longer offer me a lead. The men in the white coats and the men in the pin-stripe suits have come to take away security of home and security of work, security of family and security of faith. Some security I must have and in return for all that taking away I have been given more gadgets than a 1950s housewife and the twenty-four-hour Valium of the small screen. And you.

Why should I care? Why should you? But what then for my soul that still seeks yours?

Lengthen my stride. Let the wedding list be long. Happiness is a sandwich maker and a bed settee. What's that darling? You don't need either now that you have me. Quick open a present. Let every minute be a present, some fresh novelty we must have to forget the future and the past. I can afford it. Sell what I am, sell what I could be, sell myself to you for a gold ring. This is our last refuge isn't it? The last connected place, where for a moment you and I join hands with all the others who have joined hands and where, just for now, we make a pact with the past. Friendly ghosts will visit us but not for long. The bell tolls and we have found that every man has become an island and every woman too. Never mind, the salesman says I can call you on our mobile phone.

If everything I have become were not machine-made I might be able to take the risk of being human with you.

On top of the cake two figures feet in frost. His patent leather, her satin shoe, anchored by icing thick and deep. Beneath their tiny toes, currants and almonds, sultanas and candied peel, muscle through the white flour and halt around a sixpence. Good luck! Good luck! The bows and the bells and the tinsel and the lace, the confident Doric columns and the sugar roses in regimented rows, these will lie at last on the exhausted tablecloth, to be pocketed by the caterers for next Saturday. The little figures, totemic of a thousand tomorrows, are safe in the waistcoat of the groom.

And I? No safety without risk and what you risk reveals what you value. Sun on my face I must re-cast the bells and ring them too. I must make out of the furnace of my fears what this world is burning away. Make out of the tiny you and the tiny me, not a late Adam and Eve, but a heaven and an earth re-created. New.

A Green Square

I left my house this morning with no desire to return.

Who was in the house? My family.

Who was outside the house? Myself.

I stood looking up at the tall house in between other tall houses and I understood that I always had been outside. The insider me, the belonging me, was a dark projection on to darker walls. I am my own magic lantern, casting my body through thin air, a ghost among ghosts, lights out, wondering when the day will come.

When will the day come?

The Big Day. The Best Days of your Life. The day I was born, my birthday. Graduation Day. Pay Day. The day we met, the day we no longer met. When I take out the pocket calendar of my life I want someone to tell me where the days have gone. There are none in January. Where are my Januarys? Forty-one years of thirty-one days and I cannot remember any of them.

Is there such a thing as January? You say, 'Such and such happened.' Did it? It didn't happen to me. I watched it on a screen. I heard it on the radio. I read it in the newspaper. You told me such and such. It didn't happen to me.

Is it so unreasonable to want to play the main part in your own life? When January was showing, I was asleep at the back of the stalls, Rip Van Winkle of the snowy world. And February? And March? And April? And May?

It didn't happen to me. The lantern flickers. The light is poor. There's nothing worth watching anyway.

This January day, the woman on the bus has a travel brochure. 'Open your world' it says, and there's a photo of an aeroplane serrating the world's rim, as though the world were just another tin can.

The world is your (tinned) oyster. The packaged hygienic world with a sell-by date of Book Now.

She fingers the pearls around her neck. Her neck is dull white, English. Her pearls are brilliant white, Japanese. She pulls them round and round, like a rosary, until the cheap tin clasp is over her bosom, and the grinning beads curve behind.

She marks possible destinations with a quick Biro. India, Antarctica, Africa, Tibet.

'Don't you think?' she says. 'Don't you think?'

'What?'

'It would be nice.'

Twenty-one days a year paid holiday. I can make a note of that in August.

. . .

Where is the glittering world? I remember the salmon leaping in the Irish sea, and the wake of our boat a white triangle, in the sea sun-sphered gold.

The sea was glass, continually broken, heat-blown again into smooth panes then wind smashed. Out of the breaking and setting, the curved salmon in heraldic pairs, water-shot.

The water burned as if oil-skinned. My mouth was dry. I had drunk fire-water. My mouth was dry.

Where is the river where I was born, salmon-confident of return? Where is the sureness of an undertaking, its purpose plain, the adventure and the reason for it coded in DNA? I should have run away to sea and come back to spawn myself in my own river. I should know, instinct sharp as a fin, when the tide turns. The voyage out, the journey home, life circling itself bead by bead. Something to turn over in the hands. Something to pray for.

Prayer? Well yes. I pray as you do: 'Don't let this happen.' 'Please let it be all right.' Improvisations of need addressed to who knows where. God the horoscope column, god the tea-leaf, god the lucky lottery numbers, god when I die with the lid screwed down, this god forsaken life.

There's a man on the bus who gives out stickers saying

'Seek ye the Lord.' The woman with the brochure takes one and uses it to note her page. The Lord will be found in the Seychelles this year.

My eldest daughter has joined a tambourine sect. The kind who stamp and praise and give up cigarettes only to light up a certainty every five minutes.

My daughter wants to tell me the Truth. She knows what it is and I don't. Meanwhile my son is using her Bible for rolling tobacco. The paper is the right weight and he doesn't think she'll ever read all the way to the end. She's reading Proverbs, he's smoking Revelations.

And I am looking for the sign that says 'WAY OUT.'

'Do you come here often?'

Yes often. This fork, this point, this hesitation. I look at my house in between other houses and I wonder why I cannot accept my halter alongside the row of indentical halters that yoke us together as a society. This is how we live; house by house, family by family, pulling together along history's dirt road.

'Do you come here often?'

She means the park. The park bench that she and I share. I did not go to work this morning. I got off the bus at the park. There was a vagrant and a squirrel and a man mowing the grass and a man with a spiked stick who pierced abandoned paper cups with botanical satisfaction.

I sat on the bench without a thought, with only a great weight that would not be thought, a boulder in the cerebral cortex, my rock that I push up and down, up and down through the years of life.

When the woman spoke I assumed she was mad. We do don't we when strangers speak to us? In any case, people who sit on park benches usually are mad aren't they?

'No. I never come here.'

'Neither do I.'

'What a coincidence that we should be here at the same time.'

She looked at me oddly. She was thinking, 'This person is mad.' People who sit on park benches usually are mad.

'Warm for the time of year isn't it?' I said

'I've known warmer Januarys,' she said.

I turned to her with intense interest.

'Have you? When? Which ones? What year?'

'Are you one of those amateur weather forecasters?' she said.

The helium balloon, the barograph, the pressure sensitive needle registering the rise and fall of warm and moist, the hottest, the coldest, and all normality in between.

What could I invent to measure my changeful days? And

if I could be carefully recorded on special paper would it help? Help me, that is, to have a sense of who I am?

Never has so much been recorded by so many; the documented, identified, archival, tagged and saved world. The British Library has a copy of nearly every book written since 1840. Weather records began in 1854. Births, deaths, marriages, all there. Planning consents and blood groups. Tax returns, passports, dietary habits and driving licences. Where to find me, what I'm worth, what I watch, what I wear, my goings out and my comings in, for my security on surveillance camera. All you need to know except what I need to know: Who am I?

'Ask a silly question,' she said.

'What colour are Mickey Mouse's underpants?'

She looked pained. 'I meant, ask a silly question/get a silly answer. You're not a weather forecaster are you?'

'I never said I was a weather forecaster.'

'Are you on drugs?'

'Are you?'

She stood up. 'I'm going to call the park keeper.'

'Here, use my mobile phone.'

'You're a pimp.'

'I'm desperate.'

She started to walk away. I shouted, 'I can't walk away, don't you understand that? I can't walk away.'

. . .

Every year thousands of men and women disappear. I don't mean the ones who sell up, move away, remarry, get a job in Acapulco, go into a nursing home or mental hospital, or even out onto the streets. I mean the ones who are never seen again. The ones untraced and untraceable. Faded photographs, out of date clothes, the years piling up in the place left behind. The place where they walked away, without a suitcase or a passport, bank account untouched, appointments still fresh in the diary.

I think of a see-saw. At one end, life's accumulations, at the other end, the self. For many, perhaps for most, the balance can be maintained. The not too unpleasant ups and downs of day to day, a little loss here, a little gain there, the occasional giddy soar or painful crash.

What happens when the accumulated life becomes so heavy that it pitches the well-balanced self into thin air? All the things that I had and knew, crashing to the floor, myself shattered upwards, outwards, over the roof tops, over the familiar houses, a ghost among ghosts. I might as well be dead.

I shall be treated as dead. The dead have no rights, no feelings, the present deals with the past just as it likes. I shall become a thing of the past, worse than dead, a living dead, to be avoided or forgotten, to be abused because I shall have revealed myself as someone who can't cope.

We have to cope don't we? Get on with life, pull ourselves together, be positive, look ahead. Therapy or drugs will be freely offered. I can get help. We live in a very caring society.

It cares very much that we should all be seen to cope.

'You don't look too well dearie.' It was the vagrant in her bizarre rags, a bright blue plastic laundry bag pulled round her shoulders. She sat on the bench and flicked off the lid of a polystyrene cup.

'Hot tea. Here.'

I took it. I had seen her buy it just a moment since from the van at the park gates. It was clean and steaming and the sting of it in my throat felt like TCP.

'All alone,' she said.

'All alone.'

The boat in the Irish sea. The boat on the glittering day when I had been happy. My mind had emptied and in the centre was a clear circular pool. A diving lake I never dived in because I could never get there through the rocks and rubble of the mind's accumulations.

.   .   .

'Look at all that rubbish,' she said, watching the electric van slowly whirr from bin to bin, little men in gloves removing it all.

'They're taking it away,' I said.

'Where to?' she said. 'It just gets moved around dearie, that's all.'

If only the world could rid itself of just some of its contents . . .

The January sales. Everything Must Go. But where does it go? And when it's gone, every last steam iron and every fun-fur bikini, it will all be back again, smugly cloned in Taiwan, filling up the indecently empty shelves.

If I were Rupert Murdoch or the Sultan of Brunei I could spend my daily fortune buying more and more goods from more and more shops in a race to keep them bare. I could have bulging bodyguards armed with slim powerful credit cards, charging floor to floor, crating up their hostages on Amex.

What would I do with the silent refrigerators nobody plugs? With cascades of lingerie, unbottomed, unbreasted? With dog baskets, egg whisks, jacuzzi liners, wigs?

Could I spin the silk back into silk worms? Could I pay the ored metal back to the earth? Could I return the pine to the snow forests, the polymers to crude oil wells deep in the sea?

Load it up and send it to Mars. Why not? Deep space is a litter-garden of clapped out rockets and abandoned probes. We'll be going there ourselves soon. Human detritus on its final adventure. I'm no better than the rest. What am I but a piece of cosmic waste worth my weight in effluent?

The other day my drains were blocked. I noticed the sinister rise of flush-water in the toilet pan, and outside, by the culvert, the tell-tale mixture of paper and turds mashed into a tuna-like paste.

I cleared what I could of the flies' picnic and called out those alarming men in fluorescent vans who strap on a gas mask and fire a water cannon into the sewer. Their boots are always caked with other people's . . . overspill.

While I was waiting to rejoin the community of the sanitary I had to relieve myself in the garden. Pants down, haunch squat, out it comes, lob of earth over the lot, presto.

Meanwhile, back at the drain, strong men swam in a brown flood.

I looked at the toilet and the yards of pipe connecting it to the drain, and the yards more of pipe connecting the drain to the sewer, and the sewer itself, pipes tall as houses, carrying the end products of family life out to sea, where the same families, for twenty-one days in August, will complain of the stench of themselves.

We were in a boat and the sea was deep and clear. I've seen a photograph of the earth, copyright NASA, taken from the moon. The seas cup the world in blue. The blue-held world rested on light.

The sea is not dark and dense but banded with light, as if the light could be mined. I'm an optical millionaire, floating on gold and platinum, gold beads on the surface, pale bars beneath.

I'm as rich as a fish.

Two pounds of cod. Or a litre or fifty centimetres or whatever it's measured in these days. These days, these January days, the fish-stall in a swoon of ice, the fishman, glassy eyed.

Cod Mornay, cod crème, curried cod, cod and chips, cod battered, buttered, breaded, with beans. One thousand things to do with cod, except drop it down your trousers.

'What?' The fishman looked at me suspiciously.

'Your leaflet on cod,' I said. 'Most informative.'

'Cod is beautiful,' he said, with a vehemence that surprised me. He was raw, thick, muffled, cold, with hands lobster-blue and a wart the size of a mussel under his eye. Why should he care about cod?

'Cod's my life.'

'Your whole life?'

'Every bone.'

His wife came from out the back. She had oily skin and sparse hair and ears like flaps and her mouth was pursed in a perpetual 'O.' She wore a pale grey plastic mac and a pale mottled headscarf. She was the most cod-like woman I had ever seen.

I stared at them, standing side by side, in an aquarium of content. Whatever they had, I didn't have it, and it wasn't cod.

I moved away through the swimming crowds and passed a large poster advertising a seminar on THE LIFE WITHIN. I took out a large felt tip and wrote neatly at the bottom, Stall 4.

Why not? Weren't they Buddhas in their own way?

And here we reach the problem.

I am trying to find a way out, or maybe just an air vent, or a window, a different view that would calm and steady me against this mounting desperation. It's not too late, even though I am already half out of the ejector seat, losing my grip, breaking up, classic symptoms of a bottled life.

The problem is what to do about the problem.

I can't go to church. I'm not of the generation who simply believe. I can't put my trust in science either, whose most spectacular miracles have not been to feed the multitude on five loaves and two fishes, or to raise the dead, but to perfect mass destruction and prolong senility.

On those ratings, God is still ahead.

My knees will not permit of yoga. I do not have the frame for an orange sari or the mind of the East. I can't hear the sound of one hand clapping or find peace through twenty years of silent archery. I don't doubt any of it, but I can't do it.

The good life? Buy a smallholding and milk organic goats? Not for me. Nor a boat in the water, though it's what I go back to time and again. Perhaps that's where I should start, that image, a boat in the water.

The vulnerability of it. The insolence. Isn't that the winning human combination. Isn't that us, tumbling through the years? To suffer. To dare. Now, the sufferers don't dare and the darers don't suffer. Perhaps that's what's wrong with us all. Wrong with now, sharded people that we are.

The boat in the water. At every turn the waves threaten.

At every turn, I want to push a little further, to find the hidden cove, the little bay of delight, that fear would prevent. And sometimes I want to ride out the storm for no better reason than I need the storm. And if I die, I die, that's the gamble, the game. I cannot protect myself although I can take precautions. Society can protect me least of all. It does so by limiting my freedom. Freedom or protection. What kind of choice is that?

In the boat on the water these things are clear.

What then shall I do? Write my own programme?

I've seen nightclasses advertised in personal creativity and healing. My neighbour has joined one, and now she rolls home, week after week, with a few atrophied crayon drawings and cereal packet poems. She started these classes feeling like a worm. Now she believes she's king of the world. Is this an improvement or is it new delusions for old?

In what way am I any better? She is smug. I am cynical. She is puffed-up. I am punctured. I watch her gamely finding the energy to thrash about on life's greasy surface, while I lie paralysed, croaking about another life I think I can see.

So what is it to be? Banality of convention or banality of individuation? Shall I choose society's clichés or my own?

Is it a step forward to have understood that there is no real difference between them?

These days, these January days, one Christmas just gone, another only fifty weeks away. I take out my pocket calendar and find that important days are marked in red. How few of them there are.

Is this my lot, to move blindly on the year's wheel, accepting what comes, making nothing happen? Christmas to Christmas, holiday to holiday to holiday. Someone who strains forward because the present is so tedious and the past is a handful of snapshots?

I reached for my fat felt tip. It was green. I coloured in today's square. Today was important.

My small rise of jubilation was straightaway wetted with the thought that this was probably what people do in psycho-therapy.

'Who cares?' I said. 'The whole world's a nut house anyway.'

I walked home holding on to the green square. My little square of sea and I a boat in it. When I arrived at my tall house in between other tall houses, I was afraid to go inside. I was afraid that the tiny sliver of self I had won would be consumed again into the mass man; parent, spouse, teacher, home owner, voter, consumer, bank account number, bus pass.

But there are no solutions and there will be none. I can't get a job in Acapulco. I can't walk away. Just as I must wash, dress, feed myself every day, even though I have done it the day before, so I will have to find, every day, a green square to walk in.

Adventure of a Lifetime

We arrived in winter not knowing what to expect. What should you expect, away from home, without information, the telephone lines down and the hotels closed?

There were four of us, two men and two women, none of us married to either, each of us single or divorced. The women were better at it than us; better at the things which seem to mean nothing . . . seem to mean nothing . . . but don't.

We had answered an advertisement in a paper. 'Adventure of a lifetime,' it said. 'Send £5.'

£5. A few Euros. Less than $10. Price of a ride in Mickey Mouse or a bug infested buffet lunch at a boarded up Chinese. The risk was nothing. Why not take it? What you risk reveals what you value.

I should have remembered that the Devil comes to the farmer on his way to market, and says, 'Take this bag of gold and all I want in return is whatever stands behind your house.' The farmer knows that all that stands behind his house is a wormy old apple tree dropping Golden Delicious. The Devil can take it. This is a cinch. He hurries home swinging his swag and what should be between tree and he? His only daughter standing behind the house.

. . .

And the moral of that story is? Well, what do you think it is? To content yourself with lifting swedes when the Devil dangles his twenty-two gold carrots? Or a little warning that there's no such thing as a risk-free risk?

I thought marriage was one of those until I read the small print. I was recently divorced and all the grand gestures we made, the ceremony and neon, seem like a funfair in winter; useless, tacky, ignored. The lit-up quality of our life together doesn't work without a generator. The love has gone. So what was movement and excitement, a bit gimcrack maybe, a bit sentimental, was put into storage for a couple of years and then quietly dismantled. The Decree Absolute came through and I read the details carefully. Everything was there, nothing omitted, except that I am unhappy, which like all important things, goes without saying, I suppose. But why is that?

The important things. Where should I find them? In the detail, like God? In the risk, like the Devil?

Adventure of a lifetime. Here is the envelope. The note inside tells me to go by public transport to a place in Scotland I have never heard of and await further instructions.

Well what did I expect? What should I expect for £5? It used to be a large white note, big as a flying carpet. Think of the journeys compressed into its tissue weight. I could have ridden it like a Sultan, a princess on my pommel. I could have slept under it for a week. Then it shrunk and turned blue, nearly died I think. Then it shrunk some more, and now, almost a coin, there's nothing to be had out of it but a bag of fish and chips. The adventure of a lifetime shouldn't begin with salt and vinegar on its tail. Where are you now, my deep-fried princess?

I went to the dry cleaners to collect my clean clothes but they had been sold. I took them in before the divorce and I forgot to collect them again. Now, like most things, they are no longer legally mine. The assistant, voice like a bottle of solvent, drew my attention to the small print, as I am sure God will do on Judgement Day, and I will have to say then as now, that my eyesight is poor and I cannot reach the bottom of the optician's chart, and this will be deemed NO EXCUSE.

I am inadequate, I know, not to have read the small print, but if it is so important, one of those important things, why do they not put it in LARGE PRINT, like this, so that everyone will see how the details conspire to tell quite a different story to the plot?

So I have nothing to wear except the clothes I have been

wearing for months. In these and by bus I am expected to begin the adventure of a lifetime.

Since I was a child I have been sick on coaches. Don't you know that the riotous pattern of cloth favoured by coach firms for their seats is a direct response to the gut loads of vomit retched over them? Why else the mucky swirls picked out in carrot-orange? Why else the base-mix of brown and green?

In the stretch string compartment in front of my knees are what they call 'Courtesy Bags.' I shall be quietly filling these while everyone else is gorging themselves on prawn cocktail and Diet Coke.

The first hour went well enough until I realised that the woman four seats away was wearing my jumper. I leaned over her, casually, nicely, alarmed at her bosom, and asked her where she had got it from. The jumper not the bosom. She didn't answer me. She dug deeper with her plastic fork into the plastic flute of her prawn cocktail, the active pink prawns against her active pink chest. I felt faint, the way I do when I check my tiger wormery and see the busy pink mouths feeding on the kitchen waste.

'It is hot in here isn't it?' I said as she fanned herself with a Courtesy Bag. Hot, no wonder, swaddled as she is in a pink V-necked jumper that should be in my suitcase and isn't.

So now you are thinking that I am the kind of man who buys pink jumpers and what kind of a man is that? I wish I knew.

I slunk back to my seat and tried to write a postcard to my sister. I wanted to tell her what was happening to me but I had nothing in my hands she would recognise. Not even the jumper she had bought me for Christmas.

Risk, detail, the small print and the important things. I wrote carefully, 'Adventure of a lifetime.'

Second hour: Traffic jam. All drivers the colour of raspberries. Tried to make eyes at a strawberry blonde.

Third hour: Motorway service station. Fifteen minutes only. Tankful of diesel and fifty-six jam donuts.

Fourth hour: England spreading out before me like a *** sandwich.

Fifth hour: Courtesy Bags in short supply. Well-preserved gent lends me a jar. He's taking two hundred of them to the Mother's Union in Glasgow. They're going to fill them with home-made you-know-what.

Sixth hour: There's a smell of boiling fruit coming from the engine.

Seventh hour: Total breakdown mechanical and nervous. Coach plus fifty-six passengers stranded by blackberry hedge.

Eighth hour: Karaoke and diarrhoea.

Ninth hour: Jesus dead. The rest of us to follow.

. . .

Almost everyone and my jumper got off at Glasgow. I was left in the sticky coach that rumbled into the potted night, black and thick and shiny, until a blade of daylight scooped me out. I stood on the Tarmac, suitcase beside me, my molecules over-heated and under-slept. I was nothing. I was everything. I was all I had.

When I was a child I lost my parents early. I lost them before I had time to find anything else. Now, whenever I am quite alone, no one near me or likely to be, I feel I am back at my beginning. I feel I know exactly how things stand, the important things, at any rate.

Give away a child and you hurl a message in a bottle. There she is, your DNA, your ancient patternings, a code left for others to decipher, and you won't be able to read what you have written. You hardly know that you have written what you have written. The plot develops without you. You were the details and the risk but the story belongs to someone else.

I survived, washed up on the far shore of Bohemia, and if I have any parents, they are the kind wind and the warm soil. If I had any parents I would go to a telephone box and ring them and tell them I am scared.

. . .

The adventure of a lifetime. This is it. Cost: £5. Await further instructions.

There was a note pinned to a tree. I read it carefully. It said CARRY ON.

After a little while of carrying on, I saw a figure ahead of me, walking purposefully with a suitcase that seemed too heavy. I caught up with the figure and tapped it on the shoulder. It looked round.

'Are you by any chance on the adventure of a lifetime?' She nodded. She was small and dark with a face like a tax form. I tried to read the small print.

'Do you know where we are going?'

'No idea.'

'Carry on then?'

I started to think about Hansel and Gretel and how they found their way through the forest by leaving a trail of stones. We left nothing behind but the heat from our bodies and that soon chilled.

The moon was full and white and mysterious as a Communion wafer. Would she guide us back? Forward? I no longer knew which way I wanted to go. Pursuit or retreat. In life, ordinary lifetime life, it is so easy to march down the road until your legs finally give way and everyone crowds round the coffin and declares you did your best. You didn't though did you? The road was marked and you took it. Never mind that it was a ring road circling the heart.

. . .

'What are you hoping for?' I asked my companion.

'Nothing.'

'Nothing at all?'

'I don't want to be disappointed.'

We knocked at the door of the BIDE A WHILE guest house.

No one answered. I tried to use the phone but its cable was loose like a shipwreck and its torn off dial lay in a pool of out-of-currency shillings. No one had been here since decimalisation.

Been where? I have to say I don't know. There are no signs and we brought no maps. We were awaiting instructions. You understand don't you?

We heard a noise behind the hotel. I braved myself and went to look. There a man and a woman sheltering under some dripping ivy. They said they had been there for some years and from the moss grown over their faces I believed them. I suggested we travel on together.

'There's nowhere to go,' said the man.

'There's nowhere to stay,' I said.

He looked upset. 'This is a hotel. There's a phone box.'

'Both out of service,' I said.

'Are you a tour operator?' he asked me suspiciously.

'I'm lost,' I said. 'That's all.'

It was night. It was winter. The snow began to fall. On the coach it had been September; warm, beginning-golden, a second flush of roses, apples on the trees. I must have mislaid October as I have mislaid so much of my life. October was gold and copper and brass and then November came and locked away the gold in lead chests. I always forget, when something is here, that it won't always be here. Take it now or lose it. Risk everything.

The sky was full of torn scraps of paper, all blank. There were no instructions on the snowflakes, or if there were they melted too quickly for us to read.

Our little band went into the night and we told ourselves stories to keep warm. The stories were our fuel and food. Without them we were dead to each other and to ourselves. The usual stories were not relevant here. We had no photographs or anecdotes. Even our memories were uncertain. Testimony without corroboration is invention. There were no facts left. I looked in my suitcase; not a single one. Our bags that had been so heavy weighed nothing now. The world had seeped out of them.

We came to a clearing. The snow was on the ground but not falling. Someone had built a fire that glowed and hissed because part of it was wet wood. We were cold but we hesitated. A man came out of a rough shelter, glanced at us, but said nothing. His interest was in the fire. He had left open the door, and we moved fearfully towards it, hoping for rest or a meal. There was room in the doorway for the four of us.

Inside the hut was a baby and its mother. She held up the baby as though it were a star, five points at its legs and feet and head. The child was kicking and laughing, sparks snapping off its body and lighting up the room blue. It wore no clothing though its mother was dressed in black.

The man returned, and walking through us, gestured to the woman. She and her infant followed him out of the hut and into the clearing where the fire burned and hissed.

They took the child arm by arm, each by each, and held him in the flames, in the centre of the fire.

Far from being blackened and burned, the child's body hardened and cleared until we could see the drive of the blood through the arteries and the arteries like cobalt run through the transparent flesh. His heart was beating. He was not afraid.

My companions went forward, dream-like, trance-like into the flames. I was not in a dream or a trance and I tried to run away. There was nowhere to run. The air itself was solid. The only movement left to me was forward.

Forward towards the fire where the child held out its hand to me and I took it and let the fire catch round my trouserleg, my knees, my groin, and the child laughed and time burned round my head and I fell through the parting bars of the fire. Fell forty years through my mother's belly and into the world of men.

Psalms

If you have ever tried to get a job as a tea-taster you will know as intimately as I do the nature of the preliminary questionnaire. It has all the usual things: height, weight, sex, hobbies new and old, curious personal defects, debilitating operations, over-long periods spent in the wrong countries. Fluency, currency, contacts, school tie. Fill it in, don't blob the ink and if in doubt, be imaginative.

Then, on the final page, before you sign your name in a hand that is firm enough to show spirit but not enough to show waywardness, there is a large empty space and a brief but meaningful demand: You are to write about the experience you consider to have been the most significant in the formation of your character. (You may interpret 'character' as 'philosophy' if such is your inclination.)

This is very shocking because what we really want to talk about is the time we saw our sister compromised behind the tool shed, or the time we deliberately spat into the Communion wine.

When I was small I had a tortoise called Psalms. It was bought for me and named for me by my mother in an effort to remind me to continually praise the Lord. My mother had a horror of graven images, including crucifixes, but she felt there could be no harm in a tortoise. It moved slowly, so I would be able to contemplate the wonder of creation in a way that would have been impossible with a ferret. It was not cuddly, so I wouldn't be distracted, as I might with a dog, and it had very little visible personality, so there was no possibility of an intellectual bond, as there might have been with a parrot. All in all it seemed to her to be a very satisfactory pet. I had been agitating for a pet for some time. In my head I had a white rabbit called Ezra who bit people who ignored me. Ezra's pelt was as white as the soul in heaven but his heart was black . . .

My mother drew me a picture of a tortoise so that I would not be too disappointed or too ecstatic. She hated emotion. I hoped that they came in different colours, which was not unreasonable, since most animals do, and, when they were all clearly brown, I felt cheated.

'You can paint their shells,' said the pet shop man. 'Some people paint scenes on them. One chap I know has twenty-six and if you line them up end to end in the right order you get the Flying Scotsman pulling into Edinburgh station.'

I asked my mother if I could have another twelve so that I could do a tableau of the Last Supper, but she said it was too expensive and might be a sin against the Holy Ghost.

'I don't want the Lord and his disciples running around the garden on the backs of your tortoises. It isn't respectful.'

'But when sinners come into the garden they will think the Lord is sending them a vision.' (I imagined the Heathen being confronted with more and more tortoises; how would they know I had thirteen? They would think it was a special God-sent tortoise that could multiply itself.)

'No,' said my mother firmly. 'It would be Graven Images. If the Lord wanted to appear on the backs of tortoises, he would have done it by now.'

'Well, can I have just two more then? I could do The Three Musketeers.'

'Heathen child!' My mother slapped me round the ears. 'This pet is to help you think about our Saviour. How can you do that if you've got The Three Musketeers staring up at you?'

The pet shop man looked sympathetic but he didn't want to get involved. We packed up the one tortoise in a box with holes and went to catch the bus home. I was excited. Adam had named the animals, now I could name mine.

'How about The Man in the Iron Mask?' I suggested to my mother, who was reading her *Band of Hope Review*. She turned sharply and gave a little screech.

'I've cricked my neck. What did you say?'

I said it again. 'We could call it Mim for short. It looks like a prisoner doesn't it?'

'You are not calling the animal The Man in the Iron Mask. You can call it Psalms.'

'Why don't I call it Ebenezer?' (I was thinking that would match Ezra.)

'We're calling it Psalms because I want you to praise the Lord.'

'I can praise the Lord if it's called Ebenezer.'

'You won't though will you? What about the time I bought you a 3-D postcard of the Crucifixion and I caught you singing "There is nothing like a dame"?'

'That's *South Pacific*.'

'Yes, and this is Psalms.'

Psalms lived very quietly in a hutch at the bottom of the garden and every day I went and sat next to him and read him one of his namesakes out of the Bible. He was an attentive pet, never tried to run away or to dig up things. My mother spoke of his steadfastness with tears in her eyes. She felt convinced that Psalms was having a good effect on me. She enjoyed seeing us together. I never told her about Ezra the demon bunny, about his ears that filtered the sun on a warm day through a lattice of blood vessels like orchids. Ezra the avenger did not like Psalms and sometimes stole his lettuce.

When my mother decided it was time for us to go on holiday she was determined to take Psalms with us.

'I don't want you to be distracted by Pleasure,' she said, 'not now that you are doing so well.'

I was doing well. I knew huge chunks of the Bible by

heart and won all the competitions in Sunday school. Most importantly, for an Evangelical, I was singing more, which you do, inevitably, if you are learning Psalms.

We set off. On the train my mother supplied me with paper and pen and told me to form as many separate words as I could out of JERUSALEM. My father was dispatched for coffee and she read out loud interesting snippets from her new paperback, *Portents of the Second Coming*.

I was not listening. Practice enabled me to pour out variations on JERUSALEM without thinking. Words slot into each other easily enough when sense ceases to be primary. Words become patterns and shapes. Tennyson, drunk on filthy sherry, said he knew the value of every word in the language, except possibly 'scissors.' By value he meant resonance, fluidity, not sense. So while my mother warned me of the forthcoming apocalypse I stared out of the window and imagined I was old enough to buy my own RailRover ticket and go off around the world with only a penknife and a knapsack and a white rabbit.

A white rabbit? I jumped a little at this intrusion on my daydream. Ezra's pink eyes were gleaming down at me from the frayed luggage rack. Ezra had not been invited on this trip. I had been determined to control him and make him stay behind. In the box next to me Psalms was fidgeting. My mother was oblivious.

'When the Lord comes back,' she said, 'the lion will lie down with the lamb.'

But will the rabbit make peace with the tortoise?

. . .

Like Psalms I was feeling nervous, as one does when one's fantasy life takes control. Ezra's eyes bored into my soul and my own black heart. I felt transparent, the way I do now when I meet a radical feminist who can always tell that I shave my legs and have a penchant for silk stockings.

'I'm trying to be good,' I growled. 'Go away.'

'Yes,' continued my mother, all unknowing, 'we'll live a natural life when the Lord comes back. There won't be chemicals or deodorants or fornicating or electric guitars.' She looked up sharply at my father. 'Did you put saccharine in this coffee? You know I can't drink it without.'

My father smiled sheepishly and tried to placate her with a Bourbon biscuit, which was a mistake because she hated anything that sounded foreign. I remembered how it had been when my aunt had been to Italy and insisted on having us round to eat pasta. My mother kept turning it over and over with her fork and telling us how much she liked potatoes and carrots. She didn't mind natives or people who lived in the jungle and other hot places because she felt it was not their fault. Europe, though, was close enough to Britain to behave properly and in not behaving properly was obviously perverse and due to be rolled up when the Lord came back. Besides, the Italians were Roman Catholics. In the Eternal City there will be no pasta.

. . .

I tried to distract myself from her gathering storm by concentrating on the notices in our carriage. I took in the exhortation to leave the train clean and tidy and felt suitably awed by the dire warnings against pulling the Communication cord. Ezra began to chew it.

At last, tired and emotional, though still believing that we shared a common ground other than the one we were standing on, we arrived at our boarding house.

The following morning my mother suggested we take Psalms to the beach.

'He'll enjoy a change of air.'

I hadn't seen Ezra otherwise I might have been more alive to the possibilities of catastrophe. As it was, we made our way to a patch that wasn't too windy, said a prayer, and my father fell asleep. Psalms seemed comforted by the sand beneath his feet and very slowly dug a very small hole.

'Why don't you carry him to that rock in the breakers?' My mother pointed. 'He won't have seen the sea before.' I nodded and picked him up, pretending to be Long John Silver making off with the booty.

As we sat on the rock a group of boys came splashing through the waves. One of the boys held a bow and arrow. Before my eyes, he strung the bow, and fired at Psalms. It was a direct hit in the centre of the shell. This was of no matter because the arrow was rubber tipped and left no impression on the shell. It did make an impression on Psalms though, who became hysterical. He stood on his back legs, faltered for a moment, then toppled over into the sea.

I lunged down to pick him out but I could not distinguish between rocks and tortoise. If only my mother had let me paint him as one of The Three Musketeers I could have snatched him from a watery grave.

He was lost. Dead. Drowned. I thought of Shelley.

'Psalms has been killed,' I told my mother flatly.

We spent all afternoon with a shrimping net trying to find his corpse. We did not succeed and by 6 p.m. my mother said she had to eat some fish and chips. It was a gloomy funeral supper and all I could see was Ezra the demon bunny hopping up and down on the sands. If it had not been for my father's perseverance and devotion in whistling tunes from the War in a loud and lively manner we might never have recovered our spirits. As it was, my mother suddenly joined in with the words, patted me on the head, and said it must have been the Lord's will. Psalms's time was up, which was surely a sign that I should move on to another book of the Bible.

'We could go straight on to Proverbs. What kind of a pet would be Proverbial?'

'What about a snake?'

'No,' she shook her head, 'snakes are wily not wise.'

'What about an owl?'

'Owls are too demanding. Besides, when your Uncle Bert parachuted into the canal by mistake, it was an owl I saw just before we got the telegram.'

Death by water seemed to be a feature of our family so why not have something that was perpetually drowned?

'Let's get some fish, they are proverbial, and they will be quiet like Psalms, and they will remind us of the Flood and of our own mortality.'

My mother was taken with this idea, especially since she had just eaten a fine piece of cod. She liked it when she could experience the Bible in different ways.

As for me, I was confronted by my own black heart. You can bury what you like, but if it's still alive when you bury it, don't hope for a quiet life.

Is this what the tea board wants to know? Is it hoping to read of tortoises called Psalms?

My mother bought some brown ink and sketched Psalms on a square of stiff card. She caught his expression very well, although I still feel the burden of being the only person who has seen what emotion a tortoise can express when about to drown. Such things are sobering and stretch down the years. I could have saved him but I felt he limited my life. Sometimes I take out the sketch and stare at his mournful face. He was always mournful but maybe that is a characteristic of the species because I never have seen a jubilant tortoise.

On the other hand perhaps I never made him happy. Perhaps we were at emotional odds like Scarlett O'Hara and Rhett Butler. Perhaps a briny end was better than a gradual neglect. I ponder these things in my heart.

My mother, always philosophical in her own way, enjoyed a steady stream of biblical pets: the Proverbial fish, Ecclesiastes the hen, who never laid an egg where we could find it, Solomon the Scotch terrier, and finally, Isaiah and Jeremiah, a pair of goats who lived to a great age and died peacefully in their pen.

'You can depend on the prophets,' said my mother, when anyone marvelled at the longevity of the goats. The world was a looking glass for the Lord, she saw him in everything. Though I do warn her from time to time, never to judge a bunny by its pelt . . .

A NOTE ON THE TYPE

The text of this book was set in Centaur, the only typeface designed by Bruce Rogers (1870–1957), the well-known American book designer. A celebrated penman, Rogers based his design on the roman face cut by Nicolas Jenson in 1470 for his Eusebius. Jenson's roman surpassed all of its forerunners and even today, in modern recuttings, remains one of the most popular and attractive of all typefaces.

The italic used to accompany Centaur is Arrighi, designed by another American, Frederic Warde, and based on the chancery face used by Lodovico degli Arrighi in 1524.

Composed by North Market Street Graphics,
Lancaster, Pennsylvania
Printed and bound by Quebecor Printing,
Fairfield, Pennsylvania
Designed by Soonyoung Kwon